HAUNTINGS

THE DEVIL'S CAULDRON

"What was that?" Ned asked, awake too now. "I've been dreaming. What's happening?" He grabbed Clare's arm. "There's someone here." His hand on Clare's arm gripped her tightly, painfully.

"It's the smugglers," she said. "James Paynter and his son. They're here."

"I heard something," Ned replied. He ignored what Clare had said. "Heard a shot. Someone's hurt. They're after us."

Other titles in the HAUNTINGS series:

DAVID WISEMAN

HAUNTINGS

THE DEVIL'S CAULDRON

Hippo Books
Scholastic Publications Limited
London

Scholastic Publications Ltd,
10 Earlham Street, London WC2H 9RX, UK

Scholastic Inc,
730 Broadway, New York, NY 10003, USA

Scholastic Tab Publications Ltd,
123 Newkirk Road, Richmond Hill,
Ontario L4C 3G5, Canada

Ashton Scholastic Pty Ltd,
P O Box 579, Gosford, New South Wales,
Australia

Ashton Scholastic Ltd,
165 Marua Road, Panmure, Auckland 6,
New Zealand

First published by Scholastic Publications Ltd, 1989

ISBN 0 590 76173 0

Made and printed by Cox & Wyman Ltd, Reading, Berks
Typeset by AKM Associates (UK) Ltd, Southall, London

10 9 8 7 6 5 4 3 2 1

Chapter One

"Hi!"

The voice was warm, friendly, young, a boy's.

"Hello," she said. He smelt of salt, had come straight from the sea, for when he sat down beside her water sprinkled about him.

"Been swimming?" she asked.

He was panting a little as if he'd been running. "Yes," he said. "It's great." He had a smile in his voice. He was enjoying himself, must be on holiday like her, she thought.

"I recognized you. You're in the caravan next to ours. I saw you come in yesterday," he said.

She sat, arms clasped around her knees, turning her face to the sun. The warmth made her skin glow so that she felt content. She had not wanted to come to Cornwall when her parents first suggested it, but she was glad now they were here. The weather was gloriously warm after weeks of rain and it was pleasant to laze on the beach and to know they had

1

another ten days before they needed to return home. She lay back on the sand, relaxed and at ease with the world, and took off her dark glasses.

"Come for a swim," the boy said.

She put on her glasses again and sat up.

"No," she said, more firmly than she intended. "I promised my mother to wait here for her. She won't be long."

"Oh." She could tell the boy was disappointed. She wanted to explain but he said, "See you later then," and left her.

She was cross with herself for letting him go, letting him think she was unwilling to join him. She was a good swimmer and would have enjoyed the feel of the waves about her, but her mother would be worried if she came back from the shops and could not find her.

She should have told him. He would have understood; his voice was that sort. He would not have minded taking her hand and leading her to the water's edge. He wanted to be friendly, she could tell, and would not be upset by the fact that she was blind. And her mother would have approved of her making friends with another young person on holiday.

She turned over and lay with her back to the sun.

She knew her mother had returned before she heard her speak. "You'll get burnt, Clare. Sit up and let me put some cream on you. I got some in the shops."

Clare sat up and felt her mother's hands, cool and gentle, smoothing the cream over her shoulders. It smelt sweet with memories of other summers. Her mother put the tube into Clare's hands and told her to finish the job herself. Clare slowly spread the soft soothing cream over her skin, enjoying the heat, the

2

nearness of her mother, and the sounds of laughter coming from a family a few yards away.

"A boy spoke to me, said he was in the next caravan to ours on the site."

"That would be Ned Watson. I met him and his mother last night. He's a nice boy. Your age, coming up to fifteen."

"He asked me to go swimming with him." She paused and felt her mother's hand take hold of hers. "He didn't know."

"Of course he didn't. Come along. I'll take you over the beach and we'll find him and explain. He won't mind if I ask him to keep an eye on you. I expect you're as good a swimmer as him anyway."

"Not now, Mum."

Her mother did not try to persuade her. "I expect you're right. We ought to be getting back. It's your father's turn to make dinner. He'll get cross if we're late."

"He'll only have opened a tin of something," Clare said, but when they got back to the caravan she found her father had prepared a fresh fruit salad. She could smell the melon and the apple and the banana, all so different and so mouth-watering.

Afterwards, it was her turn to clear up and wash the dishes. It was only a small touring caravan, all they could afford, but, with the awning for her to sleep in, there was enough room for the three of them. There was a special scent to the caravan, one she could not place; it was a scent that derived from people, but it wasn't a sweaty smell; it was a scent of happiness and contentment, for her family always enjoyed their holidays in it, the freedom to do as they wanted, when they wanted, without having to answer to a hotel's time table and routine. And here, in the van, she even enjoyed washing up and the other chores that fell to her lot. Mostly she enjoyed the evenings, when the heat of the day gave way to soft breezes, and she sat outside listening to the drowsy hum of insects and the distant sound of waves breaking on the rocks. Occasionally the peace was broken for a moment by music from someone's radio but it was as quickly silenced, for most of the people on the camp site had come, like them, because they cherished the quiet of the country and its tranquil contrast to the city's bustle.

"If they want that sort of thing," Clare's father said, "they can always go up the coast to Newquay."

Sometimes on their holidays, Clare thought she would have liked a bit more excitement, but this time she agreed with her parents: no one could wish for a better, more restful, holiday than here in Polgwidden.

Polgwidden. It was an unusual sort of name, but there were so many places in Cornwall with odd names, not at all English-sounding.

"They're not English," her father said. "They're Cornish. That's something else."

"They all have a meaning, I believe," her mother told her. "Porthtowan means cove near the sand dunes, Portreath the cove with the beach. So they tell me." She sounded very uncertain.

"And what about Polgwidden?" Clare asked. But her parents seemed to be feeling too lazy to talk. Her mother sighed and Clare, from the long slow satisfied breathing coming from her father, thought he must have fallen asleep.

"Hello," she heard. It was the boy again, from the next caravan, Ned.

"Hello," she said, turning her face in his direction.

"I didn't know," he said.

4

"Didn't know what?"

He seemed embarrassed. "When I asked you to swim."

"I didn't want to swim," she said, again more sharply than she had meant.

"No," he said. "I understand."

"No, you don't."

Her father's breathing had changed. He was not asleep. He was listening to her and she felt guilty at not responding to the boy's friendliness.

"No," Ned said. "I don't suppose I do really." She thought he was moving away to his own caravan.

"Ned," she said suddenly.

His voice came back. "Yes?"

"I'd like to go for a walk. How about you?"

"Oh yes," he said. "If that's all right?"

"Come on then." She stood up, putting out her hand towards him. She felt his hand on her arm and was reassured that perhaps he did understand after all. It was a light touch, not possessive or intrusive, just there if needed.

"Which way?" he said.

"Down to the beach."

Chapter Two

When she was on holiday Clare always woke very early. At home she would lie in bed until her mother became impatient but now she wanted to be up and doing as soon as the sounds of dawn – the milkman's delivery van, the birdsong, the distant traffic – told her another day had come. She had agreed to go for a walk with Ned but she did not suppose he would be ready as early as this.

"Psst!" She heard his voice outside. "Are you awake?"

"Of course."

"Are you coming, then?"

Hurriedly but quietly, so as not to disturb her parents, she slipped out of bed, put on jeans and a sweater, unzipped the fastening of the awning and stepped into the fresh air.

It smelt good with the sweet, almost overpowering, scent of gorse, and behind that she could taste the salt in the breeze. There was already a touch of sun in the air, warm to her cheek.

"This is the best time of the day." She took a deep breath. "Come on," she said and stepped confidently forward. She knew the feel of the path under her feet. It led through a gap in the hedge down to the sand, dry gritty sand at first, far above the water line, changing after a few yards to the firm tide-washed sand that seemed to spread for half a mile or more across the bay. Her father had made a plan of the bay and its coves and inlets in the sand, so that she could trace its shape and learn something about it.

"Watch out," she heard Ned call and hesitated, putting her bare foot cautiously forward. She knew what it was. They had reached the tide line and she could smell the seaweed washed up by the sea. It must straggle along the beach with all the other rubbish that came ashore. She waited for Ned to catch up with her. She had once cut her foot on a broken bottle. She should have put sandals on, but she had been anxious to get out quickly.

"It's all right," he said. "Just a lot of seaweed and some rope and timber. It must have been a strong sea to wash all this up." He took her hand and led her through the line of rubbish until they reached the firm clean sand beyond. Clare knew the beach was empty of people. As far as she could hear, there was nothing but the cry of gulls and the slow surge of the tide a long way out. She let go of Ned's hand and ran towards the sea, only stopping when the sound of the waves told her she was within a few feet of the water.

"You frightened me," Ned said when he caught up with her. "Why did you do that?"

She didn't answer. It was lovely to run free, knowing there was nothing in her way. Beaches were

the most magical of places and this wide stretch of
sand at Polgwidden was the most magical of all. She
threw her arms wide as if to welcome it to her.

"You'm a fair pretty thing standing there like a
water sprite, m'lover," she heard a voice say and was
startled to think she had not sensed anyone's
presence. She turned to the sound, a deep, chuckly
voice that smelt of tobacco and fish, an odd, attractive
mixture of scents.

"I surprised 'ee," the man went on. "And you did
surprise me being about at this time of day when all
sensible folk be abed."

"Aren't you sensible then?" she asked.

"What me?" he said and laughed. "I be the sanest
man in all these parts, I do reckon, and the oldest
too." She could tell he was puzzled by something
about her, saw she was blind but found it difficult to
believe, from her dash across the sand.

"You do belong to be careful, m'dear." He seemed
concerned for her. She imagined him to be short and
stocky and bearded and ancient, though his voice was
strong and full of good sense.

"I reckon you be from one of they caravan things
up along."

"Yes," she said. "And you're from these parts?"

"Iss, indeed. Reuben Pascoe. That's me. You'll
have heard tell of me?"

"No," she said.

"Oh." He sounded disappointed.

"But we've only been here a day or two."

"Come away," she heard Ned whisper in her ear.
"He's a scruffy old tramp. We don't want to get stuck
with him."

"Get along then," said the man. "Your young
friend wants to be on his way." But Clare did not

8

want to go, not yet. Reuben had a good voice, not a bit scruffy, not even old, in spite of what he said about himself.

"Why are you up at this time," Clare asked, "If you say sensible folk are still in bed?"

"Whenever the tide goes out, I'm there. I do find things along the beach. Look over yonder." He stopped. "I'm sorry, m'dear, I didn't think. I've got a pile of stuff, timber and the like. 'Twas a good sea last night, a strong sea, brought up bounty a-plenty. And I do tidy the place up, make it fittin' for the likes of they tourists, such as you." She knew he had turned to go – though his steps were soundless on the sand – as the wisp of his scent left her.

"You'll be coming along to the barbecue this evening?" he called back.

"Where is it?"

"Why, on the beach of course. 'Tes always a good do. I reckon even your young friend there will enjoy it."

"Silly old fellow," Ned said, "You shouldn't encourage that sort."

"Why do you say that? What does he look like?"

"I told you, a scruffy old tramp."

"That doesn't mean anything. Is he tall, short, fat, thin, dark, bald, hairy? What do you mean, scruffy old tramp?" She was cross and turned away to walk back across the sand. It was time for breakfast anyway and it was her turn to get things ready.

"Where are you going?" Ned asked.

"Back to the camp site," she snapped.

"Then you'd better let me lead you. You'll end up on the rocks if you go that way."

That made her angrier than ever and she knew that when she was angry her sense of direction was likely to desert her. She stopped and held out her hand and Ned took it. She was grateful for the way he recognized her need for help every now and again but did not thrust it at her.

"I'm sorry," she said.

"He's short and squat and clean-shaven, wearing an old cardigan with holes in the elbows, and he's weather-beaten and beery-looking."

"That's better," she said. "Now I can see him. And I can tell *you* something. He's kind and he's thoughtful and he enjoys life. And it means nothing to me if he is scruffy. I like him. And I'll go to the barbecue and get to know him better."

The smell of wood smoke was always enticing, reminding her of the time when they had lived in the country. Now all manner of scents wafted from the beach towards the camp site, brought over by the light breeze blowing in from the sea. Clare sat raising her nose to take in the smell of sausages and charcoal, hoping it would not be too long before Ned came to take her down to the beach. There were lots of people there already for she could hear their cheerful voices, gruff and light, young and old, high and low. Sounds were lovely things, she thought, for there were so many of them and they were all so different and full of meaning.

"Are you coming?" her father asked.

"I'm waiting for Ned," she explained.

"We'll see you there then," her mother said, touching Clare's hair lightly as she passed. "Make sure you wear something warm. I expect it will feel chilly as the evening goes on." Her voice faded in the distance and Clare was alone, surrounded by a medley of sounds, confusing at first but gradually sorting itself out into individual items.

"You've taken your time," she said as she heard Ned coming over from the neighbouring caravan.

"I'm here now." He had clearly not quite forgiven her for her sharpness that morning.

"It'll be fun," she said, on their way down to the beach. "And I'm famished." The smells coming from the barbecue sharpened her hunger, making her lick her lips in anticipation. It was the beach lifeguards who had arranged the event and they were raising their voices to sell their provender, their local accents comfortably reassuring.

When they had got a supply of sausages and rolls she and Ned sat on the sand to eat. Not far away a group of young people were singing a folk song to the accompaniment of a guitar.

"Do you want to go over to them?" Ned asked, but Clare was content to stay where she was, enjoying the bustle and cheer of the whole setting.

"Well, my pretty young maid," she heard a voice say and knew it was Reuben standing before her. She patted the ground beside her. "Sit down," she said.

"If your young man don't object?"

"He's not my young man," Clare said indignantly and then was sorry. She put out her hand towards Ned and felt his cheek. "He's a friend."

"I don't mind," said Ned. "If you want to."

"Then I'll join you," said Reuben, and Clare felt his shoulder touch hers as he sat down beside her.

"Have a sausage." She offered her plate to him, and he took one and smacked his lips over it.

The singers had started on another song and Reuben sang with them.

11

"Jem Paynter was a smuggler bold,
Who sailed the Cornish sea,
To fetch the squire his brandy wine,
And bring the dame her tea.

He risked his life to run the casks,
He braved the breaker's swell,
Till one dark morn the Revenue
Did blast his soul to Hell.

The devil took his own that day,
They brought Jem home at dawn,
His body broke, his soul adrift,
His widow left forlorn.

They say he still brings casks ashore.
'Tis dreadful for to see –
A spirit running brandy wine,
And worse still bringing tea."

He ended with a chuckle. " 'Twas I wrote that, years back. 'Tes my grandson at that guitar or whatever they calls it."

"Was there smuggling here?" Clare asked. She had heard so but did not believe all the stories she had been told.

"Smuggling, m'dear? That's how poor folk lived. But 'twas no sin in those days to try to cheat the Revenue men."

"And Jem Paynter, was there such a man?"

For a moment Reuben was silent. The singers had started another refrain and he seemed to be listening to it. Then he said, "Oh aye, there was a Jem Paynter all right, but it was James. You'll find his stone in the churchyard over to the next village. 'Twas mortal

12

sad, specially so for Jos, his boy, terrible sad." He did not seem to want to say more. "I'll tell 'ee all about it another day, if you do want me to but not tonight. 'Tes a pity to spoil so sweet a time as this."

Clare sighed contentedly, her senses full of the sounds and scents and tastes of the evening, and beside her she could feel the presence of her friend Ned. He seemed contented too. But Reuben had gone, wandering away, perhaps to find someone else to provide him with a sausage or two.

Chapter Three

The next day, the weather changed, mist coming off the sea with a cold feel to it so that it was pleasanter to stay in the warmth of the caravan. But after a while Clare became impatient and sought out Ned and asked him to come for a walk. He was glad to agree. Although he hadn't said anything to Clare, she knew he did not get on at all well with his father. She had heard his father talking about Ned, saying he wondered when he was "going to do something useful for a change". Ned had heard it too and had turned away, pretending he didn't care. So, he was glad to get away from the caravan, glad to keep her company.

And she was glad to have his company. She slipped her arm into his and allowed him to set the pace. She liked the rough woollen feel to the sweater he wore against the cold. She guessed his mother had knitted it and asked him about the pattern.

"It's nothing," he said.

"Tell me about it," she insisted.

"Just dots and squares."

"Fair Isle, I expect."

"I suppose so." But he did not seem able to understand why she needed to know so much, why she was always so curious about things he took for granted.

"I want to go to the church," she said. "Let's see if we can find that tombstone old Reuben mentioned."

As they walked through the village and along the path across the downs towards the next village, St Medoc, where the church was situated, the mist began to lift and the sun struck warmly down. At times the path through the bracken narrowed so that Ned had to go first and Clare followed closely behind. The air was heavy with scents of all kinds and when they got to the crest of the ridge it was almost as if a window had been opened, so fresh was the touch of wind on her cheeks. She knew there must be a wonderful view over the cliffs to the sea, so vast was the feel of space before her.

"Tell me," she said.

"What?" Ned did not seem to understand.

"What is there to see?"

"Sky, the ocean as far as you can see, and a ship of some sort on the horizon. The mist has gone. It's going to be a beautiful day again. We could go down to the beach after all."

"We might as well go on to the church since we've come so far. I want to find out if Reuben was telling the truth."

"I don't suppose that old man knows what the truth is," Ned replied. "I wouldn't believe a word he says."

They went down the path, over sand dunes, and

eventually reached the village of St Medoc. There was a quietness in its streets, as if it was spared the invasion of holiday makers. The pavement was cobbled and once Clare slipped and had to grab hold of Ned to stop herself falling. When they passed a fruit stall, the smell of ripe peaches made her suddenly feel hungry. She paid for one each and they walked slowly on, enjoying the juiciness of the fruit, until Ned suddenly stopped.

"The church," he announced. "But we can't go any further because there's a funeral on."

Clare could hear, some distance away, the intoning of a prayer and the muttering of "Amens" at the end.

"We'd better come back later," Ned said. But it seemed the funeral was over because as they began to walk away Clare heard people come slowly from the churchyard, and then, gathering outside for a moment, talk hesitantly and finally move out of hearing. Somewhere in the neighbourhood cars started and soon there was quiet.

"Can we go in now?" Clare asked.

"There's still a man at the grave. I think he must be the gravedigger."

"Let's go in, anyway," said Clare. "I want to find James Paynter's stone."

The path through the churchyard was gravel that crunched under their feet as they walked, while Ned looked from side to side in search of the Paynter stone. "It's no use," he said. "There are so many."

"Ask the gravedigger. He should know." Clare could hear earth being shovelled, and a thin whistle coming from the man digging. She recognized the tune: it was the one Reuben had sung last night. And, as Ned led her over to the freshly dug grave, with the

16

sickly scent of lilies about it, she heard Reuben's voice greeting her. He was the gravedigger.

"It's you," he said. "I thought I recognized my water sprite."

"Do you do everything in these parts?" she asked.

"Odd jobs, like this here." He shovelled another spadeful of earth into the grave. "Sad to see her go, but she'd a good life. Courted her once, when she were but a maid." He paused and Clare imagined he must be leaning on his spade and looking back into the past. Then he said, "Come to see James Paynter's stone? I'll tek thee. This can wait a while. No harm will come to her now, I do reckon."

Clare felt a hand, large and roughened with hard work, take hold of hers. "Come along o'me," Reuben said. "And you too," he added to Ned.

She allowed Reuben to lead her through the grass until he stopped and said, "There 'tis, just as I told 'ee. Read it, young fellow. Read it aloud."

Ned hesitated and Clare could tell he resented Reuben's taking charge of things.

"Read it, Ned, please," she said. "Tell me what it says."

Ned coughed and read. "In memory of James Paynter, aged thirty-five years, who on the evening of 28 August 1814, was shot and killed by a Customs House Officer. And there's a verse but I can't make it out."

Reuben interrupted. "It says," and his voice became solemn as he intoned the verse,

"The shot struck home, his life was spent.
He to his maker swiftly went.
His cargo run, his Duty paid,
Landed at last, to rest he's layed."

17

"It's not very good poetry," Ned commented.

"It tells the story," Reuben said. "You can't want more than that."

"What happened?" Clare asked.

"Paynter and his crew were surprised by the Revenue men. 'Tes said one of the gang had tipped the wink to the Customs. Paynter was a hard case, didn't suffer fools gladly. But most of his men were loyal. Just takes one."

"What did they smuggle?"

"Anything that brought profit, m'dear, silks and brandy and even tea. There was a tax on all they things. There's a cave down along, only to be reached at the lowest of tides, called Caleb's Tea-Caddy. That's where they hid the contraband. That's where Paynter was cornered, that's where he was shot." Clare felt his hand on hers again and she went with him as he led her a few yards further along.

"This is where his son's buried. Poor Jos. Lived for years after. Never forgot that day. He was with his father, you see, when they tried to run that cargo. The first time his father had taken him."

"How do you know all this?" Ned burst in.

"Why, that would be telling," Reuben said. "And he do be seen still, wandering in the night."

"Who?" Ned sounded sceptical.

"Why, Jos, the son, but seen as a boy of fourteen, though he were nigh on ninety when he died. You can see from his stone."

Ned read aloud: "Joseph Paynter, 1800–1889."

"Is that all it says?" Clare asked.

"That's all," said Reuben. "Though there was a lot more could be told."

Ned took hold of Clare's arm. "Come along, Clare. Let's get back. I want to go for a swim."

18

But Clare wanted to hear more about Jos Paynter, the boy who had seen his father shot by the Revenue men. "Who sees him?" she wanted to know.

"Young folk mostly."

"When do they see him?" Clare persisted.

"Full moon, nights of the spring tide, such a night as Jem Paynter was shot, 'tes said."

"Why then?"

"You're mighty curious," Reuben said. "Are you always so full of questions?"

"Come along, Clare." Ned put his hand on Clare's arm but she shrugged it off.

"Have you ever seen him?" she asked Reuben.

"I did once. But get along, m'dear. Your young friend is getting restless. I'll see you later, I do suppose. 'Tes a little enough place, Polgwidden."

"I don't think you should encourage him," Ned said disapprovingly as they walked back. "Of course he's seen the ghost. On his way back from the village pub, that's when."

"I believe him," Clare said, though she couldn't have said why she believed Reuben.

"Well, I don't," said Ned. "It's nonsense."

"You didn't believe him about James Paynter and that's true, you've got to admit."

"True that he was killed by a Customs Officer, but that's all." Ned was showing his anger by rushing her along and she stumbled, catching her foot in a clump of heather, and fell.

"Ow!" The heather was prickly. She sat, out of breath and indignant at Ned's thoughtlessness, but he was contrite and helped her to her feet.

"I'm sorry," he said. "I expect Reuben is all right really."

They made their way slowly back to the camp site

in silence, Clare thinking about Reuben's account. She supposed that the story must have been told often over the years, ever since the time of James Paynter's death, perhaps with a bit added each time the tale was related, until by now it was full of rich and imagined detail. Nevertheless it was interesting and she would ask Reuben to tell her all he knew. She would have to get him on his own. Ned's presence only distracted them.

In the afternoon Ned and his family went off into Truro to shop. Clare and her parents settled for a lazy couple of hours on the beach.

It was there that Reuben found her. She wondered if he had been looking for her, for no sooner did he arrive and greet Clare's mother and father than he began to talk about Polgwidden and its past. It seemed he had already made the acquaintance of Clare's parents the evening before, at the barbecue, and they were as fascinated with him as Clare was.

"It's a lovely spot," Clare's mother said, "I envy you living here by the sea."

"'Tes calm enough now, that sea," Reuben said. "But there be times when 'tes wild as Tregenna's Bull, all froth and fury, and as mad. 'Tes dangerous then to face it, 'tes better to run for shelter. When the wind blows and the seas race you'd be surprised how different this place becomes. There be no safe harbours then along this coast, leastways no easy ones. I've seen many a ship broken against the rocks in the Devils's Cauldron."

"The Devil's Cauldron?" Clare's father repeated.

"Aye. That's the cove around the headland there. At spring tide, when the tide is out, you can get round to it if you've a mind. That's where Caleb's Tea-Caddy is, m'dear." He addressed this last remark to

Clare. "But it's not a place to seek out, save for an hour or two. And the sea's a wild and wilful thing. Like a woman." He laughed. "Uncertain. Wanton-like. Never know what she be planning."

"Get on with you," said Clare's mother and laughed.

"I'm serious," said Reuben. "At least in warning you about the sea. You folk from up-country don't respect it as we do, don't fear it as you should. I talk a lot of nonsense at times, I know, but I'm not now. You stand on the cliff above the Devil's Cauldron and you'll hear the devil roaring, the sea pounding into Caleb's Tea-Caddy, probing into every corner, seeking out the souls of dead mariners; if you have a mind to, you can hear the moaning of a dying man, and, at times, some do say, the cry for help of a wounded boy."

There was suddenly silence on the beach, no voices of playing children, no song, no laughter, not even the sound of breakers rolling on to shore. Clare was in a cocoon of stillness, created by Reuben's words, deaf to everything but the vision he had created. She shivered.

A gull screamed, a child cried, a woman called to a friend, and all was normal again, or seemed so.

"I'm sorry," Reuben said. "I didn't mean to go on so, only meant to warn 'ee to mind what you do, where you go."

"She's a sensible girl, is Clare," her mother said.

Clare sat, arms clasped round her knees, aware that Reuben was looking at her, though she did not know how she knew.

"Take care," he said. "Take care."

Chapter Four

Clare had always known she should be careful of the sea and did not go into it unless she knew there was someone near, either her mother, who was a very good swimmer, or Ned, who always stayed close to her. She knew how destructive the sea could be, but she had never thought of it in the way Reuben described it, like "Tregenna's Bull, all froth and fury, and as mad".

She told Ned what Reuben had said and asked him to go with her to stand on the cliffs above the Devil's Cauldron, so that she too could hear the wild sounds Reuben had described.

It was exactly as the old man had said it would be. As the sea pounded into the narrow cove she could imagine the sounds she heard to be the cries of lost seamen, the thundering of the waves against the rocks not quite drowning the thin wailing that came from deep below.

"Let's get away," she said. "It's horrible."

"I can see why they call it the Devil's Cauldron," Ned said. "The sea's bubbling and boiling just as if someone's stirring it madly round and round."

She could feel the spray and taste the salt even here up on the cliff and then she thought she heard a cry for help, a small voice just audible in the tumult, then lost, then heard again.

"What's the matter?" Ned asked when she turned to him and gripped his arm in sudden alarm.

"Did you hear it?" she asked.

"I can hardly hear *you* above the waves," he shouted.

"I heard it."

"What?" he asked.

But she could not explain. The sound she had imagined had already faded so that she could not recall what it was; all she knew was that it left her anxious and uneasy. She was glad when they returned to the camp site, with its happy family sounds and the smells of cooking wafting from the tents and caravans.

"Good walk?" her mother asked.

Clare did not answer; she was still under the spell of that half-forgotten cry. She wished she could place it in her mind; it had to do with something Reuben had said. But it had gone.

"Are you all right, Clare?" her mother asked.

"Yes, of course." And she was. She turned cheerfully to Ned. "This evening," she said, "I want you to come with me to find Caleb's Tea-Caddy. The tide will have gone out by then and we'll be able to get round the headland."

"Remember what old Reuben said," her mother warned her. "You can only get there for a very short time. You'll have to keep your eyes on the tide, Ned.

We don't want to have to send a boat to rescue you." She pretended to make light of it, but Clare could tell she was worried.

"We'll be careful, Mum," she said. "I won't do anything silly."

They had to wait a while that evening for the sea to go far enough out for them to get round the headland, before scrambling over the rocks on to the clear hard sand of the cove. It didn't seem like the Devil's Cauldron now.

"How long have we got, do you think?" Clare asked.

Ned thought about it for a moment. "The sea's not going much further out, so we can't have very long."

"Enough time to find the cave, Caleb's Tea-Caddy, I hope." Clare's voice echoed in the narrow inlet. Ned took her hand and together they walked up the sand and on to a shelf of pebbles.

"Is it there?" Clare asked. "Can you see a cave?"

"It's there," Ned said. "But I don't think we should go in."

"Why not?" Clare stepped on, over tumbled rocks, determined to enter the cave, even if only for a moment. "Come on, Ned. I can't go without you."

"I think it's dangerous."

"Is the sea coming in or something?"

"It'll soon be turning. We'll have to be quick."

"Let's just go inside." She reached out for him and he took her arm and reluctantly led her over the piled rocks to the entrance of the cave and a few steps inside. Here the echo was closer and Clare raised her voice in a shout to test it.

"Oh-h-h-h." The echo fell from a shout to a slow dying moan that disappeared into the recesses of the cave.

"Hi!" Clare raised her voice again.

"Hi-i-i-i," the echo replied.

"Come away," Ned pleaded.

"Away-ay-ay," the echo faded and there was a deep silence. This was where it had happened, Clare thought. It was here that James Paynter had been trapped, here he had been shot. Here that Jos, his son – what had happened to Jos?

Ned took firm hold of her arm and pulled her away. "You promised you'd take care," he said.

"Care." The echo faded as they left the cave and came into the open. The tide had turned. The sea sounded near and the salt in the air was sharp to the taste.

"Come along," Ned said and she could tell he was anxious. "I promised your mother I'd look after you."

"I can look after myself," Clare said, but she knew she needed Ned to see her safely round the headland to the main beach.

"We'll have to paddle," he said. "The water's coming in quickly." She followed him as he led her over the rocks, the sea lapping her ankles, until they reached firm dry sand beyond.

"I hope you're satisfied," Ned said.

"Satisfied with what?"

"I hope you don't want to explore that cave any more. It's not safe."

"We'll have longer later in the week when it's the spring tide. Reuben says there's time enough to go right into it then."

"Reuben!"

"He knows these parts. I've spoken to him and he says it's safe for a couple of hours at low spring tide. We can go then."

"Not me," Ned said. "I don't see the point."

"It's Caleb's Tea-Caddy." Clare explained.

"I know what it's called."

"We might find something."

"From those days? More than a hundred and fifty years ago? That's nonsense."

Clare knew he was right but her curiosity would not be satisfied until she had been right into the cave. She would go with or without Ned, she told herself, but knew she needed him.

"Please," she said and clasped his hand tightly.

"We'll see," he replied and she had to be content with that.

It was dark when they got back to the camp site and they sat in the open enjoying the evening air. Their parents were all together in Ned's caravan, a much bigger and more luxurious affair then Clare's parents could afford. They seemed to be playing some card game but not taking it too seriously for, from time to time, laughter erupted from the caravan. Ned's father was entertaining them with stories that set the women giggling and Clare's father hooting with mirth.

Ned was silent, brooding.

"What is it?" Clare asked.

"He's always like that with other people," Ned said. "I can't stand him."

Clare did not say anything. Ned's father seemed perfectly all right to her, but people behaved differently on holiday. She knew Ned had two older brothers, who were touring in Italy together. Perhaps Ned resented having to come on holiday with his parents, perhaps that was why he was so grumpy about his father.

The conversation inside the caravan had changed,

the tone more serious, so that Clare guessed they were talking about her. She didn't want to listen.

"She seems a bright sensible lass," said Mr Watson. "It's such a pity. When did it happen?"

"When she was five," said Clare's mother.

"Such a brave, adventurous girl too," said Mr Watson.

"She would worry me sick, the things she does on her own," Mrs Watson said.

"It's better that way," said Clare's mother. "Though I admit I worry at times. But I don't want to hold her back."

"That's what's wrong with our Ned." Mr Watson said. "No guts, if you'll excuse the word."

Ned suddenly got up and walked away. Clare hesitantly followed the sound of his steps towards the gap in the hedge. He waited for her.

"When shall we go?" he asked.

"Where?"

"To explore the cave, Caleb's Tea-Caddy."

"Spring tide's a day or two away, I think. You could find out from a tide table," Clare said, surprised at his change of mind.

"We'll need a flashlight. I'll borrow ours. Don't tell anyone what we are planning. They might try to stop us."

He seemed as determined to go to the cave as he had been reluctant before.

"Are you all right?" she asked.

"Of course. Why shouldn't I be?"

For much of the time Clare was content to lie on the beach, lazily enjoying the sun and the sounds of the holiday makers around them. The people who came to Polgwidden were people who enjoyed a quiet family holiday. There were no amusement arcades or fun fairs. The sea, the rocks, the sand and the sun provided the entertainment. Clare worked so hard during term-time that she liked to be left to dream and think and relax during vacations.

Polgwidden, she thought, was an ideal place for that. The next time Reuben joined her on the sand she asked him what the name meant. He thought it came from the Cornish for white pool – "Named after the Devil's Cauldron, I shouldn't wonder," he said. He had found an interestingly shaped pebble while beachcombing and put it into Clare's hands. "Tell me," he said. "Tell me what it do seem like."

Clare held it between her fingers. It was only small. She could enclose it entirely in her hand. The sea had shaped and smoothed it and as she felt it she imagined how many tides had washed it, wondering where it had broken from its parent rock.

"Well?" Reuben asked. "Does it tell you anything?"

She couldn't say. It had so many shapes to it as she turned it in her fingers.

"Well?" he asked again.

"What colour is it?"

"Blue, green, amber, black. There be so many colours there. 'Tes serpentine. So-called because it has the pattern of a lizard's skin in it."

"It feels beautiful. It has so many shapes and meanings to it. It's so old."

"I knew you understood. Keep it. It's a talisman – of good luck."

He must have stretched out beside her for after a few moments she heard a soft rumbling snore coming from his direction. She wanted to ask him to tell her more about the young Jos Paynter, but did not want to disturb him. She too felt drowsy, from the warmth and from the snoozy sounds coming from old Reuben.

"Wake up," she heard and stirred from a strange dream of grey shapes lurking in the dark corners of a huge vaulted building.

"Wake up." It was Reuben. "The tide's coming in, m'dear. You'll get wet if you're not quick." He helped her to her feet.

"There you are," she heard her mother say. "I wondered where you'd got to. The tide's come much further up than usual."

"'Tes the spring tide. And the highest of the year. Takes folk by surprise every summer," Reuben said.

"When is it at its highest – and lowest?" Clare asked.

"The day after tomorrow. Just after six in the morning is low tide. You planning something?"

"No," she replied, remembering Ned's warning to keep their intentions to themselves. "No, just interested."

"Take care, m'dear. Take care."

Chapter Five

"That's a lovely stone," Clare's mother said. "Did you find it on the beach?"

"Reuben gave it to me. He says it's a rock called serpentine."

"What does if feel like to you?"

"That's what Reuben asked me and I couldn't tell. It seemed to change shape while I was feeling it."

"Do you know what it looks like to me? A mother nursing her baby. Hold it and tell me if you can imagine that."

She and her mother often played games of this sort and sometimes Clare thought she could tell exactly what her mother meant. But this time she found it difficult. She did not think she had even seen a mother holding a baby in those days long ago when she had been able to see. She tried to remember if she had even seen a picture of one, but couldn't bring one to mind.

"No," she said. "It's just a shape, smooth and

beautiful. Reuben called it a talisman, for good luck."
She could hear her father whistling outside. He had
been to the water point to fill their water carrier. She
heard him call across to someone and Ned's father
answered. She couldn't stop herself saying, "Why
does Ned's father dislike Ned so?"

There was a pause, then her mother said, "What on
earth makes you think that?"

"We heard him last night. He said Ned had no
guts."

"Did Ned hear?"

"Yes. We didn't mean to be listening. We couldn't
help it."

"I think Ned's mother mollycoddles him. He's her
youngest. She can't let him go. And his father doesn't
think it's good for him. I expect he thinks she spoils
him." She laughed. "She thinks we're mad, the way
we let you carry on. I told her it's good for you to be so
active."

Clare was glad her mother didn't "mollycoddle"
her, had always encouraged her to do things for
herself, but had always been near to give a helping
hand.

She wanted to tell her mother about Caleb's Tea-
Caddy and her determination to explore it, but she
had promised Ned that she would say nothing. It
didn't matter; she was in good hands with Ned and
there was no danger, provided they chose the right
tide time.

When she saw Ned she told him what Reuben had
said about the state of the tide. "Early on Wednesday
morning, he said, is the lowest tide, when it should be
safe to go to the cave. Don't forget to bring a
flashlight. It won't help me, but you'll need it."

"There'll be nothing there, just a cave."

"You're not changing your mind, are you?"

"No," said Ned. "Not if you still want to go."

She could not say why it was important for her to explore the cave but she felt that somehow this would be the highlight of her holiday. When she had stepped into it the day before she had known it held a mystery, a mystery she had to solve.

"Wednesday. The day after tomorrow," Ned said, "That's the day we're leaving."

"Oh." Clare made no effort to hide her disappointment. Her parents were planning to spend another week at Polgwidden. She would miss Ned.

The next day, Tuesday, was cold and wet and Clare spent the morning reading and then playing chess with her father. Ned came into their caravan and watched for a time but finally got bored and left them. After lunch he came again. The rain had stopped and a weak sun had come out, so that Clare was happy to go for a walk with him when he suggested it.

"Wrap up well, Ned," his mother called after him. "You don't want to catch cold."

It was true, thought Clare, that Mrs Watson did fuss about Ned. She was glad her mother was not so obviously anxious.

The rain had brought out all the scents of the hedgerows, a clean fresh country smell, so that Clare felt light-hearted, but she could sense that Ned was unhappy. He did not confide in her and she did not want to probe into the reason for his misery but she felt sure it had something to do with his father. Perhaps they had quarrelled. Sometimes, when the weather was bad and families were thrown too much into each other's company in a caravan, they became short-tempered. It had even happened at times with

32

her own mother and father, though usually they were good-natured and tolerant.

"There must be blackberries in the hedgerows," she said, in an effort to distract Ned. "Help me to pick some." But he was not interested, saying there was some fruit but that it was not worth picking. She wanted to shake him out of his mood of self-pity, but, with her arm through his, walked with him along the lane in silence.

He stopped. "I'm not sure we should go into that cave," he said. "I got a funny feeling when we went there the other day, as if there were someone there who had his eye on us. Didn't you feel something?"

"Yes," Clare said. "But nothing harmful." She couldn't explain what it was she'd felt.

"Perhaps there's still smuggling going on," Ned said. "People do still smuggle, drugs and such. I got the feeling we weren't welcome."

"That's not how I felt. I can't explain it, but I felt someone there wanted my help. I know it's nonsense. How could I help anyone? What could I do? But that's what I felt."

"It was strange," Ned said. "I didn't tell you. I didn't want to frighten you, but I thought I heard someone yelling at me. I know I didn't really. The sound was all in my head. But it was there."

"I heard something too. In my head. But not anyone yelling at me. Not really. Someone afraid, I thought, someone hurt."

"An animal, do you think?"

Clare shook her head. She didn't know what it was she had heard, sounds inside her head, not outside in the cave. But real sounds, not imagined ones.

"Don't you want to go back?" Clare asked. "Is that what you're trying to tell me?"

"I'll go if you want me to. I promised."

"That's all right, then." She would not let him fail her. "Six o'clock tomorrow morning, before anyone else is up. The tide will just have reached the headland then and will still be going out. We can see all we want at that time and be safely back before anyone knows we've been away."

"If you say so," Ned said.

"It will be all right. There's nothing to worry about. And I don't suppose there's anything there but an empty cave, an empty tea-caddy."

Chapter Six

Clare reached out a hand to feel the dial of her alarm clock. She did not want it to ring and wake her parents, hoping to slip out without their knowing.

It was not yet five o'clock, too soon to be on the move, but she was restless and knew it was no use trying to go back to sleep, even though there was almost an hour to go before she and Ned were to meet. She lay thinking about the death of James Paynter, wondering why smuggling in the past seemed to be a romantic idea whereas, in the present, it was sordid and criminal. It must have been criminal in 1814 as well but so many more people seemed to be involved in those days, ordinary people, sometimes people in authority, defying what they regarded as unjust laws imposing unjust taxes.

It was no use: she would have to get up; she did not know why she was so fidgety. She slipped out of bed and put on the clothes she had made ready the night before, clothes to keep her warm in the cold of the morning and the damp tunnels of the cave. She had the feeling that the cave ran a long way into the rock, although she could not say why she had this impression. No one had told her so.

She opened the zip of the awning, afraid that its slight hiss might disturb her parents sleeping inside the caravan itself, but there was no sound from them.

The morning was fresh and she felt a moistness in the air, dampening her cheek. She drew her cagoule close about her, standing outside the caravan waiting for Ned to appear. There was a stillness all around her so that she felt dreadfully alone, with no clue to the presence of another living thing on earth. She put a hand to feel the side of the caravan to reassure herself that she was not just a disembodied being, floating in nothingness. But the earth was firm under her feet and, as she stood there, she heard the distant bark of a dog or a fox, and, not far away, a sudden flutter of wings.

She had been holding her breath and now released it with relief. She did not often feel like this. She was always receiving impressions, sounds, smells of one sort or another, but for a moment she had felt totally alone and vulnerable.

She waited for Ned, hoping it would not be long before he came, and was glad to hear sounds coming from the direction of his caravan. She heard a sleepy voice, Ned's mother's, and then a whispered reply from him. The door of the van closed and she knew he had joined her.

"What did you tell her?" Clare asked softly, taking his arm.

"I said I was going to the toilet. I think she was asleep again before I'd even closed the door. It's all right. They didn't guess."

"I'd like to be back before they get up. I wouldn't want them to worry."

"Come on, then," Ned said. "It's very misty."

"I can feel it. I hope you remembered to wear something warm. We don't want you catching cold." She laughed at her attempt to mimic his mother's concern.

"Don't you start," he said.

The sand was firm under foot. The sound of the waves told Clare that the tide was a long way out. "There's no one else on the beach, is there?" she said.

"Not even Reuben. Not a soul, as far as I can see through the mist."

They hurried across the sand and the sound of the sea drew nearer.

"Can we get round yet?" Clare asked. "Has the sea gone far enough out?"

"Hold on tight," Ned said. "We can clamber over the rocks. It's safe enough."

She held on to his hand as he led her across the rocks into the little inlet known as the Devil's Cauldron. Here the air was colder than on the open beach as if the sun were always slower to reach in here. Droplets of mist clung to her hair, so, although it was not raining, she felt almost as wet as if it were. In the inlet too there was a stillness in the air and a quiet as if the cove were cut off from the rest of the world and had an existence all its own. There was something unearthly about it. She could understand why the smugglers had made this their secret hiding place. How difficult it would be for the Revenue men to take the smugglers by surprise – unless they had an informer from among the gang.

She became aware that they had reached the shelf of pebbles at the entrance to the cave itself and, a moment after, knew from the echo that they were inside it.

"How big is it?" she asked. It felt as if it stretched a long way ahead and as if the roof were several metres high above them. She had had the same feeling when she went into Truro Cathedral with her parents the previous week. But it could not be as big a place as that, even though the echo of her voice seemed to lose itself in an immensity of space.

"How big?" she asked. "You brought your flashlight?"

Ned was silent for a moment. "The cave goes on and on," he said. "It's huge."

"What are we waiting for then?" Clare was impatient to go further in, to explore the far limits.

"You'll have to be careful," Ned said. "It's very uneven under foot, with rocks lying about everywhere."

They were slippery too, at any rate near the entrance to the cave, for as Clare stepped forward she almost fell, only Ned's hold on her stopping her.

"Careful," he said. "But it's drier further on as the cave goes up. The sea doesn't seem to reach far inside."

They climbed up over the rough jumble of rocks, scrambling as best they could. Clare had to leave hold of Ned to feel her way over the mass of boulders, guided only by his voice. The rocks were still wet but not slippery with seaweed, and the walls of the cavern dripped with water. The echo was closer as if the passage was narrowing, but there seemed no end to it.

"Oh," said Ned suddenly.

"What is it?" His voice had held revulsion..

"Some bones."

"A man?"

"No, some animal, I think. Take my arm. I'll get you over." He held out his hand to her and slowly led her past.

"How far does it go?" Clare asked, but she thought she knew the answer and was not surprised when Ned said, "On and on as far as I can see."

He stopped and said, "I'm not sure we should go much further."

"We've got plenty of time," Clare protested. "We've only been here ten minutes or so."

"It's not that," Ned said. "There's a nasty feel to the place."

"You're imagining it."

He was silent for a moment. "I don't like it."

"We've come so far. Let's go on, please, Ned. We can't turn back so soon."

"I don't know why you want to go on," Ned said and she could tell he was angry when he added, "You can't see anything anyway."

There was a long silence between them.

"All right," she said. "You go back and wait for me at the mouth of the cave. I'll come to you when I've been far enough."

"I can't leave you."

"Why not?"

"You'd get lost."

"I'm not going back, not yet."

"All right," Ned said. "But not much longer. Then it will be time to go back. The tide will be turning in another twenty minutes."

Clare was satisfied. "We'll give ourselves ten more minutes and then go back. I promise."

Ned led the way again, Clare following the sound of his voice as he described the difficulties in their path. "A large jagged boulder right in front. Keep to your left." Every now and again he took her hand and led her over an especially difficult piece of ground.

"Which way now, I wonder?" he said at one point.

"Why?"

"The tunnel divides, but straight on is very narrow and the roof very low."

"Which way is the other?"

"To the right; it's wider but a steep climb."

"Let's try that one," Clare said.

"I think we should go back."

"Just let's go on a bit more. Time's not up yet."

"If you must. I'll go in a little way first and see if it leads anywhere. Then I'll come back for you."

She heard him as he climbed up, heard the smaller stones shifting under his tread and then, echoing along out of the passage, came a cry, the crash of something falling and then Ned's voice, shrill with alarm and pain. "Clare, Clare," he called. "Clare, where are you?"

"I'm coming," she said and crawled over the rocks towards the sound of his voice. Her head struck the roof of the tunnel and she put out her hands to feel her way along.

"Where are you?" she called. "Keep talking till I find you."

"Here," he said. "Here, Clare. Hurry." His voice held terror.

"I'm here," she said. Her hand reached in his direction and she felt a foot. "I'm here. What happened?"

"I slipped and dropped the flashlight. It's gone out. Can you find it? I can't see a thing. And my ankle."

"What's the matter with your ankle?"

"I don't know. It hurts. Find the flashlight, Clare.

It's so dark. There's nothing. Say something to me. You're still there, aren't you?"

"Of course I'm here," said Clare. "Hold my hand."

"Find the flashlight, Clare. We must have it."

"I'll have to let go," she pointed out. "I'll keep talking while I'm looking. It can't be far away."

"I'm sorry, Clare. I'm not much use like this."

"Don't worry. I'll find it." She sat on the ground and spread out her arms, feeling for the flashlight.

She found it, only a few inches away, caught in a cleft between two rocks.

"Have you got it, Clare?"

"Yes," she said.

"Give it to me, quickly please."

Clare passed it to him. He breathed a sigh of relief as he took it out of her hand. "We'll be all right now," he said.

She heard him switching it on and off and on again.

"Are you there, Clare?" he asked.

"I'm here." She put a hand out and found his shoulder.

"It's done for," he said. "Broken. We're done for."

"Don't be silly, Ned." She gripped his shoulder firmly. "Of course we're not done for."

"The flashlight's broken, I tell you. I can't get it to work. We can't see a thing without it."

"You forget. I can't see a thing with it. It makes no difference to me."

"I'm sorry, Clare. I shouldn't have let you persuade me to come. I knew it was dangerous. I told you there was something nasty about this place." His voice was rising and she could tell he was frightened. It was the sort of fear she well understood. She held his shoulder tightly and drew his head towards her.

"We'll be all right," she said, as calmly as she could. "We'll get back safely. Don't worry. The only thing is, we must stop you catching cold." Again she tried to mimic his mother's tone but it seemed to do nothing to reassure Ned.

"It's not funny," he said. "Not funny at all."

She agreed. It was not funny.

"Come on," she said. "We'll have to make our way back. It's straightforward enough." She helped Ned to his feet. "Can you walk or is your ankle too bad?"

"I'll be all right, I reckon." He winced as he put his foot to the ground and leaned more heavily on Clare.

"It hurts, doesn't it?" she said. "I can tell."

"I'll manage. Don't let go, Clare. It's horribly dark."

The slope of the passage through the cave made it clear to Clare which way they should go, but their progress was slow, for every now and again Ned had to rest, the pain in his ankle making it difficult for him to continue. Clare bent to examine it. She loosened the laces of his trainer and felt his foot. The ankle joint was swollen but, though she was no expert, she did not think it was anything more than a sprain.

"Perhaps if we shout for help someone will hear us," Ned said. He raised his voice and yelled, "Help! Help!" but the only answer was the echo, gibing them, beating against the cave walls, falling and dying in a whisper.

"Let's go on," Clare said. "We'll be all right."

"Are you sure we're going in the right direction?" Ned asked. His voice was rising again on the verge of hysteria.

"I know I'm right," Clare said. "My instinct tells me I am." She couldn't explain it to Ned, but she knew they were on the right track. They could not be more than a hundred yards or so from the entrance to the cave.

Then she heard the sound of the sea and knew they were within reach of the open air.

Chapter Seven

Marion Gilbert stretched and slowly stirred. It was always good to wake up on holiday, knowing that time, so harsh a master during the rest of the year, was of no account. But it was later than she had intended to wake, half past eight. She nudged her husband awake.

"I'm going for a shower," she said. "Have a cup of tea ready for me when I get back."

He growled. "Tell Clare to do it. I'm still asleep."

Marion opened the door into the awning. "She's not there. I expect she and Ned have got up early for a walk. It's his last day. I imagine they wanted to make the most of it."

When she returned from her shower, tea was brewed and the table set for the simple breakfast they had when on holiday. Mark Gilbert went off for his shower and returned to say he had met Ned's father.

"They're angry with the boy. They told him they

wanted to leave at midday. He's avoided his share of the packing."

"I don't blame him." Marion said. "His father would make him feel he was a nuisance if he were here. I don't blame him for keeping out of the way."

"Still I'm surprised he and Clare haven't come back for breakfast."

"You know what Clare's like. She probably grabbed something to eat before she left. I wish I knew where they'd gone, all the same."

Mark Gilbert looked with concern at his wife. There had been a note of anxiety in her voice. He knew she tried to let Clare use her initiative, but liked to keep an eye on her.

"She's a sensible girl. And Ned seems to be good company for her, to know when to help her and when to hold back. She'll be all right," he said.

Marion went to stand at the door of the caravan and looked out. "It's not going to be a nice day. The weather forecast hinted at storms later. It's so changeable here."

"We've been lucky so far. We've had delightful weather." But his wife wasn't paying any attention to him. She went over to the neighbouring caravan where the Watsons were making a start on their packing.

"No sign of Ned yet?" she asked Mrs Watson.

Mrs Watson shook her head. "It's not like him to miss his breakfast. I don't know what he can be thinking about. I hope he won't be long. We want to get going before midday."

Marion Gilbert began to feel guilty. Ned's mother probably thought Clare was responsible for Ned's absence. And she tended to agree with her. Clare had an adventurous spirit that sometimes needed curbing.

That was why Ned had been good for her. He had a natural caution to match Clare's audacity. They were good for each other. She turned back to her caravan. But Mrs Watson had more to say.

"I suppose Clare is missing too?"

"Missing?" That was not the word she would have chosen.

"Well, not with you." Mrs Watson changed tack.

"No. I expect she and Ned got up early and went for a last walk on the beach together, or perhaps on the cliffs."

"Oh, I do hope not," said Mrs Watson, looking at the sky, which was now dark and threatening. "He's got a very weak chest. I'd hate him to be caught in the rain."

Marion went back into the van and sat with her husband. "She's worried about Ned's chest," she told him.

"And you? What about you?"

"Yes," said his wife. "I'd like to know where they've got to. I think I'll go for a walk on the beach, see if there's any sign of them."

"And I'll wait here. But there's nothing to worry about, I'm quite sure."

Marion Gilbert went down to the beach. It was almost deserted. In the distance she saw the figure of Reuben Pascoe, raking a line of rubbish across the sand and piling it up for burning. She walked over to him and he rested on his rake and smiled a welcome at her.

"A change in the weather," he said. "'Twill be a wild sea." He turned to face the water. "You can see it already piling up. There's a terrible force to it always but when it turns nasty that's when it claims its own. No one can stand up against it when it's in

46

this mood. You want to go on the cliffs above the Devil's Cauldron and look down. That's a terrifying sight. I've known seas there rise a hundred feet or more up the cliff. God help anyone caught in those waters."

"You frighten me," Marion said.

Reuben laughed. "You'll be safe enough in that cosy little van, you and that brave girl of yours."

"Have you seen her?"

"This morning? No. I've been here an hour or so but there's been no one, not a soul, living or dead."

"Dead?"

"Just my manner of speaking."

"If you see her, tell her to hurry home."

Reuben looked closely at her. "You'm anxious about her, I can see. But I do reckon that's one young woman who can take care of herself, howsoever she be blind. There's a girl of spirit, Mrs Gilbert, and I'd be proud of her I would."

"I am, Reuben, I am. But give her my message if you see her. Tell her to come home."

"That I will," said Reuben. He began raking rubbish together into a heap and she turned back to the camp site. The wind rose and howled about the cliffs, suddenly scattering the plastic bottles that Reuben had painstakingly gathered. He raised his fist and shook it at the sky in comic defiance.

She hoped Clare would be at the caravan to welcome her but she had not returned. Nor had Ned. Mr Watson was trying to pretend indifference but Marion could see he was no less anxious than his wife.

Mark Gilbert was standing at the window of the caravan looking at the darkening sky.

"I'm not happy," he said. "It's not like her."

Chapter Eight

The sea sounded close and with it came the taste of brine on her lips. She even imagined she felt a touch of spray on her cheeks.

"Can you hear it?" she asked.

"I can see the opening now." Ned's voice held relief. He was himself again, no longer dwarfed by the dark. "We're there." He had been holding her hand for comfort but now he let it go and she heard his steps, halting and awkward because of his ankle, moving ahead over the rocks towards the opening.

She did not move but waited for him to come back to her. She waited and wondered why he did not return. The sound of the waves, beating against the rocks of the cove, was nearer now, bringing all manner of messages to her and one, above the rest, was that it was too late. In their concern about Ned's ankle they had misjudged the time. The tide had turned – long since – and had cut them off from the beach. It would be another twelve hours or so before they could get round the headland.

"Ned," she called and her voice rang about her in the vault of the cave. "Ned," she called again.

"I'm here," he answered at last. "We can't get out. We've missed the tide. I went as far as I could, got wet through too, but there's not a chance of getting out." He sounded, in spite of the disappointment, a good deal less anxious than he had been. "I expect we'll be all right back here. We can wait until the tide turns. Come along, a bit further back." He took her hand and led her a few feet further into the cave, away from the invading sea. They sat on a rock, huddled together for comfort. It was not cold: with the sweep of the sea into the cave had come a rush of warm air.

"It'll be all right, Clare," Ned said, taking over the protective role that had been hers only a little while before. "We can sit it out."

Leaning against his shoulder, she felt a flurry of spray against her cheek and was startled by it. The sea must have come further in. "Are we safe here?" she asked.

"Perhaps we'd better move again," Ned said and drew her a few feet back. Again the sea followed them, roaring and pounding, filling the cave with sound, surrounding her so that she could have imagined herself to be drowning, so close about her was the swelling discord. But it wasn't all discord. The booming notes of the sea reminded her of a church organ, a mighty throb pulsating through the vast spaces of the cavern. It was terrifying but it was beautiful too. She wanted to ask Ned if he felt the same but once more he was pulling her further into the cave.

"It's dreadful," he said. "The noise. But at least I

49

can see something, not much, but a little. At least I can see the opening. We'll only have to wait. How far will the sea come in, I wonder?" Again he seemed uncertain.

"I'm sure we must be all right here," Clare said. "We've come back and been climbing up quite a long way. The sea can't reach as far as this."

It seemed she was right. The sound of the sea grew no louder and in fact lessened a little and only occasionally did she feel the touch of a drop of spray.

"How long shall we have to wait?" Ned asked.

"It's about twelve hours, I think."

"Are you hungry?"

Clare had not been thinking of food, had not realized she was hungry, and was sorry Ned had mentioned it, for she suddenly felt hollow, ravenous for something sweet. An orange would be just the thing, but there were no oranges; there was nothing.

"Yes, I'm hungry," she said. "But it's no use thinking about it."

"I fancy a thick juicy hamburger, piled high with fried onions, in a fresh roll," Ned said and smacked his lips at the thought.

"Oh, don't," Clare pleaded. "I was all right till you spoke."

But Ned went on, seeming to take comfort from the thought of food. "With French fries and tomato ketchup. Mmm. Followed by a large chocolate ice, topped with nuts and Cornish cream."

"No, don't, please," said Clare. "I can't stand it."

She realized that the sea had become quieter, only occasionally raising its voice in a brief sharp note to remind them of its presence.

She leaned against the rock at her back and let her head fall on to Ned's shoulder. He put his arm around her. They would be safe like this till the tide went out and they could scramble round the headland to the beach. She suddenly thought of how worried her parents would be. She had left them no message to tell them where she was going. They would have no idea what was happening, would imagine they were in all sorts of danger, whereas they were really quite safe.

"Your mother and father will be anxious about you, won't they?" she said softly. But Ned did not reply and she realized he was unconcious from pain and exhaustion. She too was tired, from getting up early and the strain of the last hour or so. She decided not to try to wake him, and as she sat quietly in the cavern, her head rolled on to Ned's shoulders and she slept too.

By midday everyone on the camp site had been alerted to the disappearance of the blind girl and her friend. The warden of the site had insisted on informing the police and a large and cheerful constable had called at the Gilberts' caravan to get details of the missing youngsters. Ned's parents had joined them and they all five sat round the small table, telling themselves they were worrying unduly.

"I wouldn't be too anxious," said P C Thomas, a young chap who looked, apart from his size, not much older than Clare and Ned. "You say they're both sensible."

"Sometimes," said Ned's father. "I wouldn't guarantee it."

"You hadn't quarrelled with them?"

"No," they all four answered in unison.

"They weren't . . ." P C Thomas hesitated, uncertain as to how to put his next question. "They weren't, sort of . . . er . . . emotionally involved with each other?"

Clare's mother looked at her husband and burst out laughing.

"Well," said the young constable. "People on holiday get funny ideas."

"No," said Ned's mother. "You can put that out of your head."

But P C Thomas was persistent. "You can never be sure about these things." He shook his head wisely. "Young people these days behave differently."

"They're good friends," Clare's mother said. "But I'm sure there's nothing more to it. And even if there were there would have been no reason for them to go off. Clare tells us everything." But, as she spoke, she began to wonder. She knew Clare, but did any daughter tell her mother everything?

"No, that's not the reason, you can be certain. They've not run away, nothing like that. They must have gone for a walk and had an accident of some sort," she added.

"Well," the young constable said, "it's true that up along the cliffs, over to the old mine workings, there are old shafts, but they're mostly well marked. There's no likelihood of them having gone exploring down one of them, is there? You tourists do get some crazy notions."

"They hadn't spoken of anything like that. They walked over to St Medoc to find some stone or other." Marion Gilbert looked at her husband.

"In the churchyard," Mark Gilbert said. "The grave of some smuggler, I seem to think."

"James Paynter," the policeman said. "I can't see any danger there." He opened his notebook, sucked the point of his pencil, and said, "I'd better have their descriptions, just to be on the safe side, though I do suppose they'll turn up as soon as I've gone. Well, how about the boy?"

Ned's father began. "Fourteen. About five foot six."

"Taller than that," his wife interrupted.

"Five foot six," repeated Mr Watson. "Thin."

"Slender," said Mrs Watson.

"Slightly built," said P C Thomas diplomatically. 'What's he wearing?"

"I hope it's something warm," said Ned's mother. "He's got a weak chest."

The constable sighed. "Anything else?"

"He's a good-looking young lad," said Clare's father. "Dark hair, brown eyes, thoughtful, dreamy. Walks with a spring. Quite strong really, even if he is slightly built."

"Sounds a nice young fellow," said P C Thomas.

"He is," said Ned's father. His wife looked at him in surprise. "Well, he is. I've never said any different."

"And the young lady?" P C Thomas asked. "What about her?"

Clare's parents looked at each other. "Here are some snaps of her," Mrs Gilbert said, taking an envelope of photos from a drawer. "Taken at the start of the holiday. We collected them yesterday. That should help." She selected three or four and passed them to the policeman. He studied them. "Ah, old Reuben, I see. Is she friendly with him?"

"Yes."

"He's a sharp old bird. I'll have a word with him. He may know something." He looked again at the photographs of Clare. "Pretty girl. Red hair?"

"Reddish. The colour's not too good in the snaps."

"Blind, you say? That should make things easier. People notice things like that."

"They might not notice Clare," said Ned's father. "You'd never know sometimes from the things she does, the way she walks. I admire her. And you too," he said suddenly to Clare's mother. "The way you encourage her." He turned to the policeman. "You'll find her and Ned? Won't you?"

"Don't worry, sir. They'll turn up safe and sound, I'm sure."

Chapter Nine

She woke with a start and yet she wasn't sure she was awake. She thought she had been dreaming but was not sure what had broken her dream or what it had been about. But she knew now what was keeping her on edge, alert to danger. There was movement somewhere in the cave – furtive movement . . . low voices . . . mutterings . . . a command . . . the tumble of something wooden that made the echoes ring.

"Fool!" a man said, the word deep and threatening. Then a shout brought her sharply to her feet, a loud cry, followed by a warning, "Get away, get away." The echoes of the cry were drowned in the thud of feet on rocks, a confusion of yells, then a moment of dread silence during which Clare sensed someone brushing past her, a rush of cold air, and then another shout ringing through the hollows of the cavern, rising, falling. "James Paynter," the cry boomed. "James Paynter. We're coming in. You've no way out, no way out." The words spread about her, touching her, riffling through her hair, seeking out the man James Paynter.

She heard a sigh, close to her, and knew if she put out a hand she could touch him. A whisper came, almost into her ear. "Make yourself scarce, Jos. Go up along. They'll not find you. They won't think of looking for you." There was someone else, on the other side of her. "No," a young voice said. "I'm not going."

"You'll go," the older voice said. "I'll face them alone. Go now. Do as I tell you."

She knew the presence had left her, the older man. She heard his footsteps, slow and measured, tread away, and heard other steps, light and secret, follow after.

"Paynter," a bellow came from far away and filled the space around her. "Paynter. There's nothing you can do, can do, can do."

"I'm coming. You can take me. 'Tes all up, I know. I'm coming out."

There was a laugh of triumph, another voice calling, "Paynter! 'Tes all up with 'ee, now, now, now." There was a malevolence in the voice that made Clare shiver with revulsion. Then Paynter called, "I did reckon 'twas thee, Penrose. You'll never prosper for it. How many pieces of silver did they pay 'ee? 'Twill do 'ee no good, no good, no good." The echoes had barely died away when there was a shout of alarm, a shot, a scream and then a fusillade of shots that burst into the cave and echoed around them, as if the very bullets were ricocheting from the walls, whining and shrill, and in all the noise a soft moaning and the cry of a boy, "No, father, no!" There was another single shot, another cry of pain, this time, Clare knew, from the boy.

She shuddered with fear, for herself as well as for the boy. Silence fell, to be broken by the sound of steps cautiously entering the cave, silence again, followed by a whispered, desperate plea, "Go, boy, go. 'Tes no use. I'm done for."

She felt something, someone, stagger past her, then halt and turn, hesitate, move forward, turn again, as a voice called. "So, James Paynter. We've got thee now. 'Tes no use struggling. Drag him forth."

Clare heard a sob held back and choked off.

"What was that?" Ned asked, awake too now. "I've been dreaming. What's happening?" He grabbed Clare's arm. "There's someone here." His hand on Clare's arm gripped her tightly, painfully.

"It's the smugglers," she said. "James Paynter and his son. They're here."

"I heard something," Ned replied. He ignored what Clare had said. "Heard a shot. Someone's hurt. They're after us." He turned as if to run and she put her hand out to stop him.

"We're imagining it," she said.

"What?"

"The sounds, the shots, the cries."

"I can hear them," Ned said. "I'm not imagining anything. There's someone here." He pulled himself away from her. "Someone touched me."

"Where are you?" Clare asked. "Where've you gone?"

"Come on," he said. "They're after us and they've got guns."

"Ned," she pleaded. "It's nothing." But she seemed to be speaking into space. Ned had gone, getting away from the sounds that still seemed to fill every corner of the cave, shouts and cries and the moaning of someone in mortal pain.

"Come away," she heard Ned call. "Come away."

She scrambled on all fours over the rocks in the direction from which his voice had come. Someone touched her hair and she thought it was Ned and put out her hand to reach for his, but there was nothing there. "Jos," she said, for she knew it was him, but there was no answer but a sigh and a soft gasp as if the boy was in pain. He's been wounded, she thought, and I can do nothing to help him. She stretched out her hand and touched a foot. "Ow!" came Ned's voice. "That hurt."

"I'm sorry," she said and scrambled up to sit beside him.

"What happened?" he asked.

"I don't know."

"What made you scream?"

"I didn't scream," Clare said, but she wondered if, in her fright, she had done so.

"I heard you. I was sleeping, dreaming, I think, and you woke me. I thought someone was after us, thought I heard a shot, but it was all a dream. Where are we?"

"In the cave. Where do you think?"

"I know we're in the cave, but where in the cave? I could see something before, but it's all black now."

"You clambered up here. I followed you."

"I can't have done. I'd remember." He sounded puzzled. "You're there?" he asked. "Give me your hand."

She reached out to him and held his hand.

"I don't like this," he said. "I'm not really a coward, Clare, honest. I just get a weird feeling in the dark. Let's find our way back to where we were before."

They moved down a little way, slowly because neither wanted to lose contact with the other.

"Are we there, do you think?" Clare asked. "Where we were?"

"I can't see anything."

Clare could not hear the sea as she had before, the steady swish and wash of the water against the rocks of the cave. They seemed to have come to a totally different part of the cave system. How had it happened like that? In their panic, at the strange sounds, they must have entered another tunnel. She put out a hand and touched a wall of rock.

"Where are we?" Ned asked and his voice held a terror that echoed Clare's fear. "We're lost." His voice began to rise in near panic, then he seemed to take control of himself, breathed deeply, clasped Clare's hand and said, more calmly, "We're lost, aren't we?"

Chapter Ten

They *were* lost, with no idea where they had got to; all they knew was that they had left the cave far behind in their flight from some imagined horror.

"Can you hear anything? The sea?" Ned asked.

They sat quietly, hoping to hear a ripple, a splash, the sound of waves, anything to point their way back to safety, but there was nothing, nothing until . . .

"What's that?" Ned whispered.

"You heard it too?" Clare said, straining to make sense of it – laboured breathing only a few inches away, a gasp of pain, a sob.

"What is it?" Ned asked again.

She held her breath, listening closely, then she felt movement near by and put out her hand but found nothing. Again she heard a sound, a quick catch of breath, and knew what or rather *who* it was – Jos, the boy of Reuben's story. Jos, who had seen his father murdered by the Revenue men. Jos, who was here, needing help and comfort.

"What is it?" Ned said again.

"Who is it, you mean? Can you see him? Anything?"

"I can't even see you," he said with sudden anger, an anger that hid the fear he was trying to control. "Keep near me. Let me have your hand," he pleaded.

She heard a long soft sigh, felt a touch of warm air against her cheek – not Ned, but someone else slumping to the ground beside her, leaning against the rough rocks of the tunnel wall. It was Jos and she felt a deep pity for him. He had seen his father killed and now like them, he was lost in the darkness of the cave.

"You'll be all right," she whispered. "I know you will."

It was Ned who answered. "I hope so. But nobody knows where we are. They won't know where to look."

"We'll find the way out."

"The way out," an echo came from beside her, as if Jos had spoken. "The way out." She felt him move and knew he had got to his feet. She heard him wince with pain.

"Come on, Ned," she said and, taking her friend's arm, dragged him after her.

"Where are you going?" he began and resisted, but she pulled him on. They had to keep up with Jos, follow him wherever he went. Jos knew his way through these passages and would lead them to safety. "I know this is right," she said. Jos moved slowly but confidently ahead as if he were familiar with every twist and turn of the caverns.

They stumbled after him, feet slipping from time to time, elbows scraping against the rough walls.

"Please," Ned said. "Stop a moment. My foot hurts."

Jos had stopped too and was leaning against the rock wall. Clare could not see him, not even in her inner eye, but she knew he was there as certainly as if she could see and touch him.

And she could touch him. She put out a hand and felt a mop of curly hair, damp and unruly. She pictured him, shorter than Ned, but broader, with thick-set arms, strong. She reached out to feel his cheek and let her hand wander over his face so that she would know what it looked like. His lips curled upwards indicating good humour, his cheeks were round and full and his chin was firm. As she touched him she felt a hand cradle her chin and fingers reach to her lips and follow the line of her mouth.

She knew what he was like and liked what she knew. She wished she could really have known him and then realized she did know him, all that was important to know. He was brave and self-contained, and his courage and determination would save him – and them.

"Jos," she whispered and heard a slow sigh in return as if he understood.

"Keep hold of me," she heard Ned say and his hand reached for her arm. "It's awful in the dark. Not seeing you or anything. It's almost as if I'm not here, not anywhere, unless I have you to hold on to."

"We'll get out, Ned. Jos knows the way."

"What are talking about?"

"Jos is with us. Can't you feel it?"

"Jos who? You're crazy."

"Jos Paynter. I've heard him. He's here, with us. You heard him too."

"It was a rat or a bat."

"A boy," Clare said, "A boy. Jos Paynter. He's here."

He put his hand down to his ankle where the bullet had nicked him. He could feel the blood seeping from the wound and needed to halt every few yards. From time to time he became faint with pain and with fear that he might never escape from here, might wander through this maze of passages for all time. But, whenever he felt near despair, he heard a small voice urging him not to give up hope. Sometimes the voice was in his head, sometimes in the air beside him, but wherever or whatever it was it gave him fresh heart so that, after a brief rest, he was able to move on.

He heard her now and, feeling her touch, thought his mind was wandering from the loss of blood, making him imagine the presence of some guardian angel. But she was there with him, whatever she was, urging him on. He lifted himself up and dragged himself along on all fours, trying not to put weight on his injured foot. He tried to work out how far he had come and how far he had still to go. He wondered if his memory of the cave system was false.

Then he recognized where he was. Here and there, to help them pull their loads along, smugglers before his father had driven handholds of iron into the rock face. His hand touched one now. He tried to grasp it to haul himself upright but had not the strength. He slumped back against the rock and felt and heard no more.

"Are you there, Clare?"

Clare moved cautiously towards Ned's voice. She caught her head on a jagged piece of rock and felt the blood trickling down her forehead. It clotted quickly so the cut could not be very bad, she decided.

"I'm here," she said. They sat, leaning against each other, holding hands, desperate not to lose contact.

"How shall we ever get out?" Ned asked. "Where does this lead? No one will have any idea where we are." He was trying not to show how afraid he was, keeping his voice light and steady, but Clare knew he was terrified.

She was terrified too from time to time, as now. It was as if Jos had left them and she and Ned were on their own. She had felt confident before that they were on the right track, following Jos, certain he would lead them to safety.

She trusted him to find his way out – and to point the way for them. But there were times when her courage and her trust began to fail her. She thought that was when Jos himself was uncertain, when he too began to doubt if he would get back alive.

He had got back alive. She knew that, for he had gone on to live to a ripe old age. She had seen it on his tombstone in the churchyard at St Medoc. They only needed to follow him and they would come to safety.

But where was he now? She had lost him. There was no one at her side but Ned, no sound from Jos. He had left them; she and Ned were alone in this vast labyrinth. She caught her breath, but quickly suppressed a burst of panic. With or without Jos she would find her way out. Mere dark held no terrors for her; she was used to it. Yet she was frightened, she could not help herself.

She tried to speak cheerfully. "Come on, Ned. We mustn't give up." She pulled him to his feet. "We'll find a way out, don't worry."

She felt a hand take hers, but it was not Ned's. Jos had come back to her, had taken hold of her and was leading her slowly out of the passage into a wider cavern; she could tell the roof was high from the empty echo of their footsteps.

"It feels different," said Ned. "Where are we?"

They stepped forward and lost contact with the walls at the side. Clare stretched a hand out to touch the rock but felt nothing. Only the rough and tumbled stones at her feet and the grip of Ned's fingers at her wrist brought her into contact with reality. Ned held her so tightly that it hurt but she did not say anything. She understood his feeling of helplessness, his need to hold on.

Jos had gone again.

She had lost him. "Jos," she said softly and the whispered echo came back at her. "Jos." But no more than an echo.

"Jos," she called again, louder this time, but there was no more answer than the mocking sound of her own voice.

"Why do you keep calling 'Jos'?" Ned asked. "There's no one here but us."

"He's here, somewhere, I know. At least he was. He wants to help us."

"Don't talk like that. I think you're going crazy. Try and be sensible." He took both her hands and held her close to him. "We'll get out, Clare. I know we will." He was trying to show a confidence she knew he did not feel.

"Yes," she said. "I know we will too." She put her hand to Ned's cheek. They stood holding each other for a moment, both afraid but neither wanting to admit it. "We'll get out, of course we will," she said firmly.

Chapter Eleven

"Have you any news?" Clare's mother looked hopefully at Reuben as she opened the door of the caravan to him.

"I came to ask about them," the old man said.

"You've not seen them then?" Marion Gilbert let her disappointment show.

"Not since yesterday."

"I can't imagine what they're about."

Reuben rubbed his hand through his sparse hair, "'Tes puzzlin', that's so. But I shouldn't worry overmuch. She's a sensible young woman. Sees more, in a manner of speaking, than many a sighted person. You can be proud of her."

"That's no comfort to me, I'm afraid, Reuben. She's still very vulnerable, however sensible she may be." She invited him into the caravan to have a coffee.

"This is about the eighth cup I've had already this morning," she said. "Where can she be, Reuben?

You've talked to her. You must have some idea what she and Ned have got up to."

"I've racked my brains, such as they be, to imagine where they might have gone. She was very interested in my stories. I did tell her all sorts. But 'twas my tale of James Paynter and his son Jos that seemed to interest her most."

"What about them?"

"How they were smugglers, caught by the Revenue men in Caleb's Tea-Caddy."

"Caleb's Tea-Caddy?"

"The cave round the headland, in the Devils's Cauldron, the next cove. But . . ."

"But what?"

He hesitated. "Most times it's cut off by the tide. I suppose 'tes just possible they went out there this morning at low tide and got caught. If they did, they'll be quite safe so long as they stay put above the water line. But . . ." Again he paused. "If they do go wandering off further into the cave – well, it do go a long ways back, a proper maze of tunnels and passages and old mine workings."

Clare's mother put her hand to her mouth in horror. "Now that won't have happened," Reuben hastened to say. "I tell 'ee, that girl of yours has too much sense to go wandering off into the unknown. I don't know about the boy."

"Ned's not the sort to do anything foolish."

"Then that be all right then. Come low tide they'll appear safe and sound round the headland, hungry as gannets, but none the worse apart from that."

"Is there nothing we can do if they are there? Can't we get a boat round?"

Reuben shook his head. "They're unkindly waters in the Cauldron, but even if we got round there we'd not be able to get into the cave till the tide falls and that's not till half past six or so this evening."

"It's a long time." Marion Gilbert sighed. "I can't bear the waiting." She looked hard at the old man. "What is it, Reuben? What are you thinking?"

"Nothing, Mrs Gilbert. Just anxious, like you." But he was remembering a day when he had gone into the cave – a day like this at spring tide – and had seen things beyond the imagination. He did not believe in ghosts, even though he told stories about them, but the mind could play strange tricks and in a cavern lashed by a wild sea, a young blind girl and an impressionable boy might hear all manner of things, might well have been driven back into the web of caves in retreat from some imagined fear – or from some spectre from the past. Once it had almost happened to him.

"What is it, Reuben?" Like her daughter, Mrs Gilbert was sensitive to people. She knew he had thought of something.

But he couldn't tell her. She was worried enough, he thought. He laughed. "Don't take on, Mrs Gilbert. That girl of yours will be fine. Whatever sort of fix she's in, she'll find her way out, never fear." And suddenly Reuben felt sure the girl would be safe and that maybe he could do something to help. He had family papers at home, diaries, plans of the old mines, Jos Paynter's work. He would go and examine them. He couldn't sit idly back while the girl might be in danger. There was something even an old codger like him could do.

Chapter Twelve

Jos was on familiar ground now. Though his father had not let him take part in the landings on the beach before, he had helped in the carrying of contraband from the Tea-Caddy up through the workings to the surface. He thought he knew his way but twice he had lost it in the confusion of old mine passages. Now he had got back to the main chain of paths, taking the girl with him. He did not ask where she came from; he was merely glad she was there and had courage, a courage which fed his, and which helped them both. He wondered what she was doing here. He thought the caves were known only to his father's men. Where had she come from? Where was she going and who was this with her? Someone much less real than the girl, it seemed.

He wanted to ask her who she was, but though he tried to make himself understood she did not answer him, only saying his name from time to time. How did she know his name? The whole thing was very puzzling. He wished his father were here to help him understand. But his father was dead.

He must not think of that; when he did, his courage failed him and he lost his sense of direction and even the wish to escape. He must get out quickly, reach his mother before they brought his father's body home, be with her to help her over the shock.

He had stopped to rest for a moment and now stretched, sighed and got to his feet. He felt the girl rise with him and follow him. Once again he wondered if he was imagining things, if perhaps he was seeing a ghost. The caves were haunted by "buccas", spirits who worked the mines, the little people. But this girl was no "bucca"; she was real. He was puzzled but he was not frightened, not of the girl. And even if she was a spirit she meant him no harm. She gave him the will to live, to make his way out of here.

He must keep a clear head for the difficulties before him. He was coming to the gunnis, a huge cavern, long since worked out of its tin. From here three drives opened, only one of which, as far as he knew, led to safety.

He left the girl at the opening into the gunnis and found his way across. He would come back for her when he had found the rushlight and the tinder that was left in the drive beyond. Then all would be well. There would be no more false turns, no hesitations, just a straight passage to the surface and safety for himself – and for the girl. He thought he heard her call his name and turned round but in this intense dark he could see nothing. He made his way by instinct across the working and entered the drive. This was the one, for he gripped another iron handhold driven into the rock. Just beyond, in a hollow in the wall, he would find the rushlight and

70

the tinder box, wrapped in oil paper against the damp. He felt his way forward. It would be there for he had seen his father put it there. Again the thought of his father made him pause, almost drowning him in despair, but he forced himself to think of his mother and her need of him.

He put his hand into the hollow and groped around, found the packet, drew it out, felt for the steel and flint and tinder and struck a spark. It took. He touched the glowing tinder to the rushlight and slowly its faint illumination lit the drive, casting weird weaving shadows about him. He put the tinder box back in the rock cranny and strode on, with more confidence now. He would soon be out.

He had forgotten the girl until, from the gunnis he had left, came a cry for help, his name called once, twice. He turned hurriedly in answer, tripped and almost lost hold of his light. His foot disturbed a rock at the side of the drive; the stone and the one above it shifted and he held his breath, but they seemed to settle safely and he went on, out of the passage, to answer the call. He held the rushlight forward and in the dim light saw two figures standing in the middle of the huge chamber, vague shifting shapes, there at one moment, lost the next.

Then, from the passage he had left there came first a slow tumble of rock, then a sudden cascade of sound, a flurry of wind that blew out his light and a storm of dust that made him catch his breath and fall to the ground, choking on the powdery cloud that fell about him.

She was alone, the echoes of a rock fall ringing in her ears, the taste of dust in her throat. She stretched out to touch Ned but felt nothing. She called his name but for a moment there was no answer, her voice lost in the noise of the tumbling stones.

"Ned!" she called again, trying to control her terror. "Where are you?"

"Keep talking," he answered. "I'll find you."

"Thank heavens," she said. "I wondered what had happened to you." She felt a hand touch her shoulder. "Is that you?" she asked.

"Who do you think it is? Of course it's me. What happened?"

The dust had settled and there was silence, broken only by a cough and a sneeze from Ned. Clare began to wonder if they would ever reach the open again, but she would not let herself doubt, could not give up hope. Yet, without Jos to guide them, they did not know which way to turn.

And where was he? Had he left them? Had he had an accident? That wasn't possible. He had got out of here, she must remember that.

"Jos," she called. "Jos. Where are you?"

She felt a hand at her elbow, but it was Ned, holding her tightly, making sure they did not lose contact again.

"Jos," she called, raising her voice so that the echoes rebounded from the walls and ceiling in a bedlam of discord.

She felt another hand and knew it to be Jos touching her, reassuring her that he was there, ready to lead her and Ned to safety.

"Oh, Jos," she said. "I thought you'd gone." She felt his hand, rough and firm, take hold of hers, and courage returned, flowing from him to her and back again.

"We'll be all right now, Ned," she said. "Hold on."

Ned did not speak. She wondered if he sensed Jos was there. How could he not know? The presence of Jos was as clear to her as that of Ned, his touch as real.

She followed where Jos led, slowly, stumbling a little from time to time on the uneven surface but never losing contact with him and with Ned's hand on her shoulder. Jos seemed in no doubt of the way.

The sound of their footsteps changed and she knew they had left the huge echoing emptiness of the cavern and entered a narrow passage. Occasionally she brushed against one or other wall. It was a passage that rose in a steep incline. Pebbles rattled beneath their feet and every now and again Jos stopped, let go of her hand and seemed to be shifting rocks or stones that lay in his path. Each time she felt lost and was relieved when she felt his hand reach for hers again. She gripped his fingers fiercely and he responded by holding her as tightly.

"Don't leave us, Jos," she said. "You'll get out. We'll follow you. We'll all escape."

He did not speak in answer, or if he did, she could not hear him, but she knew he was taking heart from her confidence in him.

They went on, moving easily at times, but at others crawling awkwardly over heaped stones, with barely room to pass. Then she almost lost touch with both Jos and Ned. Once she was entirely on her own until Jos reached out a hand to drag her forward, and Ned came bumping into her, falling over a pile of rock.

"Clare," Ned said. "I must rest. My foot's hurting. Are you there?" His voice raised in fright.

"I'm here," she answered and sat down beside him where he had slumped to the ground.

Jos had stopped too and was sitting on the other side of her. She could feel his shoulder against hers and put out a hand to touch the rough cloth of his jacket. How solid he seemed. Yet how could that be? She must be dreaming, her mind hazy with hunger and weariness and fear. Yet he was real to her, as real as Ned.

Her hunger was real too, a yearning for something to eat so strong that her mind was filled with images of the sausages she had enjoyed at the barbecue. She could taste the fried onions. But it was an illusion, of course.

Perhaps this was *all* an illusion, a dream. Maybe she was really asleep in her camp bed under the awning of the caravan with her father and mother sleeping a few feet away.

But it was not a dream, she knew. There was something nightmarish about it, but it was real, the rocks under her feet, the water dripping down the walls and the rough feel of Jos's jacket.

She felt herself dropping off to sleep and knew she must try to keep alert. But the air was close in this narrow passage and she fought against her exhaustion. Ned's breathing told her he had already gone to sleep. Perhaps she should shake him awake, get him to move, but she had not the energy, and Jos too seemed to want to rest. Her head drooped and she let herself go.

Chapter Thirteen

Reuben Pascoe sat in the living room of his little cottage overlooking the beach, thinking about the girl Clare, wondering where she and her friend Ned might have gone. He suspected they had ventured into Caleb's Tea-Caddy and been trapped by the tide. He was beginning to regret having told Clare so much about the smugglers and Jos.

If that was where they were they would be safe enough if they stayed put until the tide went out. Clare would know that was the sensible thing to do. They would come walking out of the cave, safe and sound, as soon as the water receded. There was no need to worry.

He was worried nevertheless. He had once been caught in the same way sixty years back. His young mind had filled the cave with all manner of ghosts. It had been the same time of year, he remembered. There had been a full moon and a spring tide, which had tempted him to round the headland and venture into the cave. Freak waves and a rolling sea had cut him off before he realized it.

And then, then . . . He recalled so vividly what he had seen: a powerfully built black-haired man, standing defiantly at the opening of the cave, and behind him, almost lost in the shadows, a young boy. He had heard a shout and a volley of shots, had seen the man fall and the young boy dart towards him and then turn and run, stumbling once, clutching his leg, and then make off, disappearing into the gloomy recesses of the cave. Curious, and surprisingly not frightened, he had followed the boy for a while and then, coming to his senses, had halted and gone back to the main cave to wait for the tide to turn.

He had mentioned the incident to his father when he got home. His father had looked strangely at him, not disbelieving as he expected him to be, but nodding sagely.

"Have a look at this, boy," his father had said. "'Tes my grandfather's writing, your great-grandfather, Joseph Paynter. Read it." He had read the pages then with growing amazement.

He took them out now, his great-grandfather's account of his life from that day in 1814, when he had seen his father killed, to a few days before his death in 1889. It was years since he had looked at it.

The paper was brittle and yellow with age. At the start the writing was ill-formed, as if the boy who wrote it was unused to handling a pen. Later the penmanship became florid and confident and then, towards the end, crabbed and wavery. But the account was always strong and compelling. It had formed the basis of many of Reuben's own stories to visitors.

He sat, holding the sheets of paper without

reading, trying to picture his great-grandfather. The only photograph of him showed a stocky figure in a frock coat. The pose was stiff but in his eyes was a dreamy expression as if he were looking, not into the camera, but into the past – or even into the future.

He had something to tell, something about the cave that was important. And what he had to tell was somewhere in the account of his life, somewhere round that awful time of his father's death. Reuben leafed throught the sheets of paper, then began to read, but he was interrupted by a knock at the door. He went to see who the visitor was.

"Why, Mrs Gilbert!" he said. "Come along in. You've got some news?"

Chapter Fourteen

She could hear voices, wild wayward voices, a horrid jumble of sound echoing and booming within her head. She shook herself awake. Ned was calling, his voice frenzied with alarm.

"Clare! Clare. Where are you?"

For a moment she wondered where she was. She had been thinking of the caravan, its warmth cosy with the presence of her parents. Where was she?

"Clare!" Ned's voice again, taut with panic.

She remembered then where they were, deep below ground, lost in a warren of tunnels. "I'm here Ned," she whispered. She hadn't even strength to raise her voice. She felt stiff, knees aching from the awkward position she'd been lying in. She should not have let herself go to sleep. She must keep alert.

"Where?" Ned repeated.

"Here," she said and heard him moving towards her. He reached out for her and she took his hand and held it.

There had been someone else with them, she recalled, but who? Then memory flooded back. Jos had been with them, Jos Paynter, the young boy. "Jos!" she called softly, then more loudly, "Jos." But there was no answer. Somehow she knew there would be none. He had gone, had found his way out and left them to save themselves. The presence which had been so real before – the boy, the guide, the helping hand – had gone.

Yet, if he had gone, finding his way to the surface, they too could follow and escape. They had been moving along the narrowing passage steadily upwards and following Jos until weariness overcame them and sleep had brought forgetfulness. She thought Jos had rested with them. He must have wakened before them and gone on, to find his way to the surface.

"Come on, Ned." she said. "This must be the way." But, without Jos to guide them, her confidence was faltering.

She crawled along on hands and knees, uneasily aware that the walls and roof were closing in on her. Then she found she could crawl no further. The passage was blocked by rocks large and small. Was this the way Jos had come? Had the rocks tumbled after he had got through?

Perhaps he had not got through. Perhaps the Jos Paynter who was buried in St Medoc churchyard was another person altogether. Perhaps her Jos had been buried beneath the fall. For a moment despair clutched at her so that she wanted to lie down and give way to weariness and hunger.

"Jos!" she called, once, twice, but there was no answer.

She felt Ned's hand on her shoulder. "Why have you stopped?" he asked.

She was silent for a moment, finding it difficult to tell him. "It's blocked. The passage comes to an end. There's no way out here."

"Then we must go back," he said. "There will be other passages." Ned seemed to have found a new source of strength, though his voice wavered a little.

"Yes. We must," she said. There was nothing else for it. She wondered how much time had passed since they had come into the cave, twelve hours, a day, two days and two nights? Her hunger made her think it had been a long time. They should have brought something with them, a bar of chocolate, anything.

"Come along, then," Ned said and she heard him move away, whistling to keep his courage up. She did not like the sound. It seemed unearthly, as if it came not from Ned, but from spirits wandering the mine passages with them, spirits who wished them ill. And soon Ned stopped, as if he too found the sound unnerving.

Slowly they retraced their steps and after a while, as the passage widened, they were able to stand upright. Then they became aware, from the difference in the echoes, that they were in the huge cavern again.

"Stop," Clare said. "We don't want to get lost in the middle. Let's keep close to the wall. We'll find another exit from it. I'm sure."

But she was not sure any longer. With Jos there she had felt safe. Now that he was no longer with them, she was all too aware of the weight of rock around and above them, pressing close on all sides.

"Hold tight," Ned said and clasping hands they moved slowly around the rough-hewn walls of the gunnis, tripping on the uneven floor, disturbing pebbles, sending stones tumbling from the sides, their breath catching in the dust they raised as rocks cascaded at their touch. She was afraid that at any moment their clumsy movements would start a rock fall that might bury them alive.

One or two rocks fell, but nothing more. Ned led the way and she followed, holding on to his anorak, stepping warily, as they felt their way round the walls of the cavern.

Ned stopped. "There's a passage here," he said. "Shall we risk it?"

"We must," she said. "What else can we do?"

They left the echoing vastness of the cavern for the close confines of the passage, Clare leading the way, at first walking upright and then crawling on all fours as the walls drew tight about them, the rock scraping at their backs as they wormed their way forward.

Jos stood, glad to stretch to his full height. He took great gulping breaths of the clear air, fresh even here at the foot of the shaft. He could see the circle of blue sky above and on the walls of the shaft a metal ladder to the top. He mounted it, slowly because of the stiffness in his arms and the pain in his foot. He had made it. He had known he would; when at times he had begun to despair he had heard that voice telling him he would be safe. He looked round, half expecting to see her behind him, but saw no one. And no one could follow him for, as he had moved along the passage to safety, he had dislodged a jumble of rocks that had blocked the way. There was no escape for anyone else by that route.

He felt a sudden guilt. He had left her there, her and that other, in the depths of the workings, left her to find her own way out. And who was she? How could she have walked with him, spoken his name, known who he was? He could not understand, thought perhaps the terror of the last hours had made him delirious, or worse, driven him mad. Such things happened, he knew. How could there have been anyone there? He had been alone when his father had been killed.

The memory of what had happened to his father came sharply back, so that in his misery he threw himself to the ground at the top of the shaft. Once when he was a small boy he had wandered away from home to this very shaft and climbed down the ladder to see what was at the bottom. His father found him, hours later, and beat him for his folly. He recalled the beating so clearly, wished his father could come to find him now, would not mind the beating he deserved.

He sat up and wiped his eyes. Never again would his father put out a hand to him in anger or in love. Never again. He got to his feet and staggered away towards the village. Once he turned back, thinking he must not leave the girl. Without his help she would remain there, lost in the workings for ever. He could not let that happen. There must be a way out for her too.

Chapter Fifteen

"I can't sit around doing nothing," Mrs Gilbert said. "How soon can we get into the cave?"

Reuben looked from his window to the sea. " 'Tes not far off now. We should be able to get round in half-an-hour or so. Let's go and gather the others."

They went to the camp site and collected lanterns, blankets and a thermos of hot tea and then Reuben, the Gilberts and the Watsons made their way across the beach to the headland. The sea had calmed a little but dark clouds massed on the horizon, threatening storm.

"I'll lead the way," Reuben said. " 'Tes familiar ground to me."

He knew, as soon as he reached the cave and swung his lantern around, that the place was bare. There was no sign of the youngsters, no trace of their ever having been there. He feared the worst: that they had been startled by something and had wandered off, only to lose themselves in the twists and turns of the old workings.

"Well?" said Clare's father. "What do we do now?"

Reuben saw they were appealing to him. He made no answer. He was listening in the vain hope that there might be a sound, however slight, giving a clue to the youngsters' whereabouts. But there was nothing, only the sea and the wind outside and, at his elbow, a sob from Ned's mother as she flung herself into the arms of her husband.

"Now, now," Mr Watson said. "There's no need for that." But his voice too held a note of despair.

"Perhaps they were never here at all," said Clare's father. "We're only guessing."

"They were here," said Marion Gilbert suddenly as she stooped to pick up a small stone from among the pebbles at her feet. "Here, Reuben. Do you recognize it?"

He took it from her and nodded. "Yes," he said. "The stone I gave her. I called it a good luck talisman, I remember."

"Good luck!" said Ned's father angrily. "A lot of luck it's brought!"

"At least now we know they were here," said Mr Gilbert. "It gives us somewhere to start."

"We musn't take too long," said Reuben. "We don't want to be caught too."

"I'm not giving up now," said Mr Watson. "We know they were here. We've got to try and find them."

"There are other ways into the workings," said Reuben. "It's too dangerous to stay here with the tide coming in. We'll be no use to them if we get caught as well, or if we get lost in the caves."

"What can we do?" Clare's mother turned to him.

"Trust me," he said.

"Trust that old fool," Mr Watson said under his breath, but Reuben heard him.

"Trust me," he said again. "And my great-grandfather," he added.

"I think the man's mad," Mr Watson snorted, making no attempt this time to keep his voice low.

"You'll see," said Reuben and led the way out of the cave just in time to avoid their being cut off by the advancing sea. The Watsons and the Gilberts followed him, not the least bit reassured by Reuben's apparent confidence. They watched as the old man turned off to his cottage. Marion Gilbert made as if to follow him but her husband took hold of her arm and led her back to the caravan.

Chapter Sixteen

Reuben Pascoe had not been off his head – as Mr Watson thought – when he mentioned his great-grandfather. Jos Paynter had known the cave system thoroughly, had come out of it safely on that dreadful day in 1814 when his father had been ambushed, and had explored it often afterwards.

Reuben had left the yellowed sheets of old Jos's writings on the table. He picked them up and began to read, handling the papers carefully. The family had always been proud of the old man and the story he had written was precious to them.

Reuben read: "My dad is dead. I saw him killed by a Revenue man. It was dreadful. I was frightened and ran away and thought they would follow me but they stayed with my father. I saw them drag him out of the cave and knew he was a goner. They fired a shot into the cave and hit me but I was not badly wounded though it hurt.

"My mam says I should try to put it all behind me.

But I see my dad whenever I close my eyes. I should have helped him. I ran away."

He was only fourteen, Reuben thought. What could a mere boy have done? The Revenue men would have shown him no mercy. He had been right to run. He could not have helped his father, and his mother needed him. Reuben skipped through the story, anxious to get to the part where Jos had found his way out. That might give a clue as to how he could help Clare and the boy.

Some of the account of Jos's escape had been written a long time afterwards, when Jos was older and had been back to the caves and the mine workings. He seemed to feel a compulsion to explore them. He had drawn detailed plans of the system, marking caves and adits and shafts in neat copperplate writing.

"I found my way to the drive at the foot of Hoskin's Shaft but there was a rock fall blocking the way. I thought I was done for at first but a voice kept telling me to keep on going. I don't know who it was but I would have given up but for that voice telling me I would get out in time.

"But it was hard. My foot hurt and I had to stop and rest a lot and I got hungry. I thought of Mam's pasties and that made me feel worse. Once I went to sleep and when I woke up I thought I was dead. I had forgotten where I was. It was all so dark. I wonder if that's what dying is really like?"

Reuben skipped a bit more. His eyes lit on the words "Mason's Shaft". This was it.

"I missed my way once and took the wrong turning but went back and found another drive. It was almost blocked with fallen rock but I managed to crawl over it and then saw, high up, a small blue dot. It was the sky. It was Mason's Shaft. I had found it and I was safe. I scrambled to the foot of the shaft and as I did so rocks began to tumble down. I thought at first I was done for but when the rocks settled I was all right. I could still see sky. But behind me the way out was blocked. Blocked. I tried to clear a passage but it was no good. There was no way out by Mason's Shaft for anyone after me."

Reuben put the papers down. His hand was shaking. No way out, he read. But he refused to believe it. There were other shafts, other adits, other drives. The earth was burrowed with old men's workings. One would surely lead to grass. He picked up the papers again.

"I cannot rest till I have found another way," Jos had written and the plans showed how carefully he had surveyed the workings, naming every feature. Wheal Dawn, Wheal Friendly, West Shaft, Johnson's Shaft, Mason's and Prior's, they were all there. And one was marked in Jos's careful hand "This way is open." Prior's Shaft.

"This way is open." But was it still? There could have been many more rock falls since Jos had explored the workings. And where was Prior's Shaft? The ground was riddled with old shafts, most of them half filled with rubbish, thrown down them by the cottagers over the years. He studied his great-grandfather's plans carefully, trying to match them with a modern Ordnance map of the area. On the Ordnance map many spots were marked "old shaft" and one, on the cliffs above the camp site, seemed to correspond to Jos's placing of Prior's. But who could tell, after all this time, if the way was still open?

Reuben realized how much time had passed in his perusal of Jos's papers. It would soon be light and time to go to the camp site to join the search party. And now he was armed with information provided by his great-grandfather. So much for Mr Watson's disbelief!

Chapter Seventeen

She had not wanted to sleep but was too tired to resist the impulse to lie down and close her eyes. It would be so easy to lie here and give up hope and get gradually weaker and weaker. Her legs ached and her knees and hands were sore from scrambling over the stones; and they had no idea where they were going.

She woke, startled, aware that someone had touched her. Not Ned, for she could hear him snoring softly a foot or so away. "Jos?" she said, not daring to believe it was him. "Have you come back?" It was Jos, she was certain, though he did not answer. He had come back for them.

She reached out to Ned and shook him.

"What is it?" he said grumpily, then "Oh God! We're lost, aren't we? And no one knows where to look for us."

"We're not lost," she said. "I know which way to go." They had stopped to rest at a division of the ways. The passage they had climbed along veered right and seemed to be wide and level, but to the left was a narrow channel, barely wide enough for them to enter.

"It's the wrong way," Ned said as Clare now squeezed through into the left-hand passage, but he followed her, desperate not to be left behind. As she scrambled along she could hear him grumbling away behind her.

The passage rose in an incline and with every step Clare imagined she felt a breath of air, fresh and cool, touching her brow. That meant hope; it meant escape.

But progress was often slow and difficult. At times the way seemed wholly blocked by boulders and fallen rock. She could feel the great rough stones piled jaggedly where they had fallen from the roof of the drive. She managed to crawl over them, head touching the rock above her and elbows scraping against the walls at her side. Once she thought she was stuck but managed to wriggle her way through.

"Don't leave me, Clare," Ned pleaded, for to get over the rock fall she had to let his hand go. "Keep talking so that I know you're still there."

Instead of talking she began to sing what she could remember of Reuben's song about Jem Paynter. She hoped Jos would not mind, She was sure he was beside her, not saying anything, not even leading her by the hand, but somehow entering her mind, giving her fresh heart. "Jos," she whispered, hoping he would see how glad she was he had come back.

She took a deep breath as she scrambled over the piled rocks. The air again felt fresh and cool. She called to Ned. "We'll soon be there."

"Where?" he said. "Where?" His voice was still anxious, unconvinced. "We should have gone the other way."

"Can't you feel it?" she said, knowing suddenly they had not far to go. "Can't you feel the cold air? We must be nearly there. We must be."

She crawled further up the passage and stopped to listen, but all was silent, save that for a moment she imagined she heard the cry of a gull. But how could she hear a gull's mew so deep underground?

Deep underground? Perhaps it was not so deep. She felt a little flicker of hope.

"Can you see anything?" she said to Ned as she felt him scramble past her, and seemed to wait ages for his reply.

"Yes," he said slowly. "There's a faint light ahead. I don't believe it." He raised his voice in a shout. "It's true. There's light in front of us. Hold my hand, Clare. I'll help you. There's light. There's light."

There's light, Clare thought and turned to thank Jos for leading them to safety. But he was not there to thank. He had brought them but had gone now, gone for good. She knew she would not meet him again.

With each step the air became fresher, sweeter. Suddenly Ned stopped and Clare bumped into him. "What is it?" she asked.

"We're at the bottom of a shaft," he said. "I can see blue sky. It's magic." His voice was filled with relief. "We've made it," he said. "I knew we would. I told you so."

Clare smiled. She was tired, more tired than she had ever been. She almost felt like weeping with joy. Later perhaps she would give way, but not now, not till she was alone.

"Right," she said. "Lead the way."

There was no answer.

"Ned. What is it?"

"I can't see a way up. There's a bit of an old metal ladder or something but it doesn't go far."

"No way up?"

"Not that I can tell. But at least we can see the sky." His voice was exultant. Coming out of the dark of the caves he had recovered from the black despair that had threatened him before. She was glad for him, glad he could see the light above.

"How do we get out?" she asked. "How deep is it? Can we climb up?"

She could tell Ned was studying their position, gazing up the shaft, searching the walls for climbing holds.

"Well?" she said after a while.

He was silent then at last he said, "We'll have to shout for help. Someone will hear us. It's daylight and there are bound to be people about."

They raised their voices together. "Help!" they called, "Help! Help!", and the words rose up into the shaft and faded into the air above. A gull screamed.

Chapter Eighteen

On the camp site everyone was stirring. Clare had become known to all the campers and they were concerned for her. They were worried about Ned too but, after all, they told themselves, it's so much worse for her since she's blind. They were eager to start searching.

Marion Gilbert comforted Ned's mother, reassuring her that all would turn out well in the end, though she did not feel as confident as she pretended.

Clare's father had gone to see P C Thomas to ask if there was any news. He came back shaking his head. "But he's coming to organize the search party."

"A whole night in the cold," said Ned's mother. "I don't dare to think how poorly he'll be."

Her husband took hold of her hands. "He's a lot stronger than you imagine. He'll have come to no harm."

They had none of them had much sleep and had been up and about at first light, hoping the youngsters would have turned up of their own accord. The two fathers had gone again to the cave but had decided there was nothing to be done, not until all other efforts failed.

There was a knock at the caravan door. "It'll be P C Thomas," Mr Gilbert said. But it was not. It was old Reuben.

"Well?" said Ned's father impatiently. "And what did your great-grandfather have to tell you?"

Reuben smiled. "You'd be surprised."

They could hear voices outside, men, women and children assembling to form the search party to scour the countryside for the blind girl and her friend. "Maybe we'll get somewhere now," Mr Watson said.

They joined the other campers and Reuben followed them. P C Thomas organized them into groups and put the local men in charge of the parties that were to search the cliffs and the coves along the coast.

"Ah, Reuben," the policeman said when he caught sight of the old man. "Have you come to help?"

"Him and his great-grandfather," muttered Ned's father, not quite under his breath.

Reuben smiled again, that slow knowing smile that seemed to make Mr Watson even angrier.

"I'll just go up along," Reuben said. "Up along the downs to Tregenna's farm."

"Why there?" asked the policeman.

"His great-grandfather told him," Mr Watson said. One or two of the campers sniggered but Clare's mother said, "I'll come with you, Reuben."

"And so will I," said her husband.

"Let's go then," said P C Thomas and the groups set off on their different ways, with the Gilberts, and, surprisingly, the Watsons too, following Reuben.

The sun had risen and the early mist had gone. A clear duck-egg-coloured sky, free of cloud, promised a bright day.

Reuben strode purposefully on, swinging an old walking stick, pushing aside nettles and brambles in his path.

"Maybe he does know where he's going," Mr Watson whispered to his wife. He seemed to be changing his mind about the old man.

Chapter Nineteen

They had become hoarse with shouting and all to no avail, for it seemed as if the world above had emptied of people. They were beginning to feel faint with hunger. Clare could not imagine how long it was since she had last eaten. They sat close together, backs against the wall of the shaft.

"How deep is it?" Clare asked.

Ned thought for a moment. "At least forty feet. Perhaps more."

"Is there no hope of climbing it?"

"I might have a go. I might manage to find a foothold here and there. I'll have a try. It's no use just sitting here. There doesn't seem to be anyone about to hear us."

"Be careful, Ned," she said.

"Don't worry, Clare. And don't fuss. You're as bad as my mother."

She was glad he had quite recovered from his recent terror. How many hours had they been down here? Time below ground had dragged so that as much as a couple of days might have passed. Perhaps the light Ned saw was the fading light of dusk. Perhaps they would have to spend a long night at the bottom of this shaft.

There were no sounds to give her a clue as to the time of day. Down here all she could hear were the scraping of Ned's shoes on the rocks as he climbed and his muttered curses when his foot slipped. Then a stone fell, dislodged from the wall, and he came tumbling down, banging into her where she sat.

"Damn," he said. "It's no use. The sides are all crumbly. I could bring the whole lot down on us."

"Are you all right?" she asked, thinking of his sprained ankle.

"No, I'm not all right," he said angrily, then laughed. "Of course I'm not all right. Are you? Sitting here, cold and hungry and wet. You do ask silly questions." But he was cheerful about it so that the damp and hunger seemed bearable.

"Food," he said. "Think of it. Hamburger. Steak. Bread and butter pudding. Scones and jam and cream."

"Stop it," she said. "Stop it." Her mouth began to water. "Let's try shouting again."

They called for help, cupping their hands round their mouths and yelling up the shaft. "Help! Help! Halloo!" they called until, dismayed at the lack of response, they fell silent, thinking they must be miles from any cottage or any path along which people might pass.

"Can you tell from the light what time of day it is?" Clare said.

"It's brighter than it was."

She hoped that meant the day was at its beginning.

At least if hours of daylight were left someone might come by.

"Let's play a game," she said.

"What sort of game?"

"Anything to pass the time."

Ned was not enthusiastic, but she persisted.

"The Minister's Cat," she said. "I'll start." She thought for a moment. "The minister's cat is an archbishop and his name is Artaxerxes."

"You do make it difficult," Ned said.

"Your turn," Clare insisted.

"The minister's cat is a blackguardedly cat and his name is Beelzebub," he said after a moment.

Clare thought hard before she spoke. "The minister's cat is a classical cat who catches crickets and caterpillars and confines them in a cage and keeps then in captivity till Christmas."

"You cheated," Ned said. "Keeps begins with the letter K. And what's his name?"

"Her name," she corrected. "And her name is Cleopatra."

Soon their stories of the minister's cat had developed into lengthy accounts of fantastic feline lives, as each of them added to the other's sentences until they fell about in laughter, for the moment forgetting their situation. By the time they came to the letter R they were hysterical.

Clare had begun, claiming it was her turn. "The minister's cat is a rude, rumbustious rotund ruffian of a cat who runs riot through Redruth."

"Me now," said Ned, "running round and round in ragged raiment, reeking of rotting rhubarb and ripe rice pudding."

"And his name is," Clare began, and they both yelled, "Reuben!" They roared with laughter and yelled again, at the tops of their voices, "Reuben. His name is Reuben!"

"I thought I heard something," said Mr Watson, who had wandered away from the others, dissatisfied with Reuben's slow and cautious progress through the brambles and bracken.

"You be careful where you tread," Reuben called to him. "There be old men's workings all over to these parts. You never know where they might be. And I do reckon the shaft we want be somewhere hereabouts."

"I heard something too," Mrs Gilbert said, standing still. "Didn't you?" She turned to her husband.

"Quiet, everyone," Clare's father said. They stopped where they were and listened.

"There, I told you," Mr Watson said excitedly. "There again."

From somewhere near at hand there came the sound of laughter, followed by a shout – a boy's voice and a girl's – of "His name is Reuben!" Hoots of mirth rose in the morning air. "His name is Reuben!" More laughter.

"It's them," said Mark Gilbert. "Clare!" he called. "Ned!"

But the laughter had stopped and a silence followed so that they began to wonder if they had imagined the whole thing.

"Where did it come from?" Mrs Watson asked anxiously. "Where?"

"Listen," her husband said. And they heard Clare's voice, no longer raised in laughter but slightly quavering, seemingly only a few feet away, saying, "Shall we carry on?" and Ned's answer, "It's not helping, is it?"

"Clare!" her mother called. "We're here. Keep talking till we find you."

"Mum?" The voice came from the left of them, from somewhere within a circle of stone, a wall marking a shaft, overgrown with heather and almost collapsed from the passage of time.

"Careful," said Reuben. "Let me." Prodding with his walking stick at the ground in front of him he approached the shaft cautiously and peered over.

"Hello, you two," he said.

"His name is Reuben," said Clare tearfully.

"'Tes all right, m'dear," Reuben said. "We're here. You're safe now."

Chapter Twenty

Her mother took her to Reuben's cottage on the hillside and left her at the door. She still felt stiff and her knees and elbows were still a bit sore. She could smell the ointment her mother had put on to help the grazes to heal.

"You're both very lucky," Clare's mother had said. "It could have been so much worse. I dread to think what might have happened."

"Don't go on, Mum." Clare begged. "Don't get like Ned's mother."

"It's only that we love you, you know. You can't guess how hard it is to let you have your head."

"We were quite safe, Mum, honestly." But she remembered the terror that had seized her from time to time, aware that it was only the knowledge that Jos Paynter had managed to get himself out that had kept her courage up. Had they really been saved by a ghost? All she knew was that someone had guided them through the caves and workings to safety. She had known then it was Jos, had spoken to him, touched him.

Ned did not understand her. He had forgotten how frightened he had been when he imagined the shouts and shots which had driven him away into the dark. He couldn't recall why he had panicked. She didn't remind him. But she knew what she had heard, would never forget it, could even see it in her mind's eye.

Reuben had been watching out for her and led her in. "Sit here, m'dear," he said and took her to a chair by the open window. She could smell the brine from the incoming tide and could hear the roar of the breakers against the cliffs below the little house. It felt safe and secure here, warm and comfortable, in the way that Reuben himself was.

"So, tell me all about it," Reuben said after he had brewed tea and put a plate of chocolate biscuits near Clare. She took one, crunching it hungrily, as if she hadn't eaten for weeks. She felt like making up for lost time.

"Well?" said Reuben.

"How did you know where to look for us?" Clare asked.

"Ah," said Reuben. "I had my sources."

"Your great-grandfather, Mr Watson said, but he was being funny," she said.

Reuben was silent for a long time.

"My great-grandfather," he said. "You're right. Jos Paynter. That's who it was."

"Yes," said Clare. "That's who it was."

"He was there?" Reuben asked, but it was less of a question than a statement, as if he knew Jos had been with her in Caleb's Tea-Caddy, as if he knew he had led her to safety.

"I wish I'd known him," Reuben said. "But I did

see him once. Many years since." He paused and Clare heard him move his chair away from the table. She knew he had come to stand near her to look out of the window. "Down there. Like you. In Caleb's Tea-Caddy, for a moment. I can see him now, a young boy. 'Tes strange that."

"What did he look like?" Clare asked. She longed to know if the picture she had worked out in her mind was the true one.

"I don't rightly know," said Reuben. "But I reckon I do take after him, broad and solid. A bit shrunken and wrinkled with age now, but when I was a lad. . ." His voice drifted away as if he were looking back on those times.

"When I was a lad," he said after a while. "But I'm not a lad any more. I saw him then." Clare heard him removing the cups from the table, but he stopped and said, "You saw him too?"

Yes, she thought, perhaps I did. Perhaps what I imagined in my inner eye was the real Jos, the boy who escaped from the Revenue men to become an old man, but whose spirit returned to the place where he had seen his father killed.

How could it be? She could not tell, but it had been so, and she was sitting here in safety in proof of it.

The sounds of Polgwidden came to her through the window, the swell of the tide against the cliffs, a quarrel of gulls screaming raucously on the sea wall, and the laughter of children on the beach.

"I'm glad I met him," she said without thinking.

"So am I," said Reuben. "So am I."

HAUNTINGS by Hippo Books is a new series of excellent ghost stories for older readers.

Ghost Abbey by Robert Westall
When Maggie and her family move into a run-down old abbey, they begin to notice some very strange things going on in the rambling old building. Is there any truth in the rumour that the abbey is haunted?

Don't Go Near the Water by Carolyn Sloan
Brendan knew instinctively that he shouldn't go near Blackwater Lake. Especially that summer, when the water level was so low. But what was the dark secret that lurked in the depths of the lake?

Voices by Joan Aiken
Julia had been told by people in the village that Harkin House was haunted. And ever since moving in to the house for the summer, she'd been troubled by violent dreams. What had happened in the old house's turbulent past?

The Nightmare Man by Tessa Krailing
Alex first sees the man of his darkest dreams at Stackfield Pond. And soon afterwards he and his family move in to the old house near the pond — End House — and the nightmare man becomes more than just a dream.

A Wish at the Baby's Grave by Angela Bull
Desperate for some money, Cathy makes a wish for some at the baby's grave in the local cemetery. Straight afterwards, she finds a job at an old bakery. But there's something very strange about the bakery and the two Germans who work there. . .

The Bone-Dog by Susan Price
Susan can hardly believe her eyes when her uncle Bryan makes her a pet out of an old fox-fur, a bone and some drops of blood — and then brings it to life. It's wonderful to have a pet which follows her every command — until the bone-dog starts to obey even her unconscious thoughts. . .

All on a Winter's Day by Lisa Taylor
Lucy and Hugh wake up suddenly one wintry morning to find everything's changed — their mother's disappeared, the house is different, and there are two ghostly children and their evil-looking aunt in the house. What has happened?

The Old Man on a Horse by Robert Westall
Tobias couldn't understand what was happening. His parents and little sister had gone to Stonehenge with the hippies, and his father was arrested. Then his mother disappeared. But while sheltering with his sister in a barn, he finds a statue of an old man on a horse, and Tobias and Greta find themselves transported to the time of the Civil War. . .

The Rain Ghost by Garry Kilworth
What is the secret of the old, rusty dagger Steve finds while on a school expedition? As soon as he brings it home, the ancient-looking knife is connected with all sorts of strange happenings. And one night Steve sees a shadowy, misty figure standing in the pouring rain, watching the house . . .

The Haunting of Sophie Bartholomew by Elizabeth Lindsay
Sophie hates the house she and her mother have moved to in Castle Street. It's cold and dark and very frightening. And when Sophie hears that it's supposed to be haunted, she decides to investigate . . .

Picking Up the Threads by Ian Strachan
There's something strange going on at the rambling old house where Nicky is spending her holidays with her great-aunt. In the middle of the night, Nicky is woken up by the sound of someone crying for help. But when she goes to investigate, there's nobody there!

The Wooden Gun by Elizabeth Beresford
Kate is very unhappy on the Channel Island where she's spending her summer holidays. She senses a mysterious, forbidding atnosphere, but no one else seems to notice it. Is it just her imagination, or does the beautiful, sun-drenched island hide a dark secret?

The Devil's Cauldron by David Wiseman
Although Clare is blind, she lives her life to the full, and is never afraid of taking chances. So when she is told about the old smuggler's cave, she persuades her friend Ned to come with her to explore it. But the cave holds more than just memories of the violence it saw many years ago . . .

HIPPO BESTSELLERS

You'll find loads of very popular Hippo books to suit all tastes.
You'll be in stitches with our joke books, enthralled with our
adventure stories, in love with our romances, amazed at our
non-fiction titles and kept amused for hours with all our
activity books. Here are just a few of our most popular titles:

A Dark Dark Tale (picture book) by Ruth Brown	£1.95
Postman Pat Goes Sledging by John Cunliffe	£1.75
Little Tiger Get Well Soon (picture book) by Janosch	£1.95
Bambi (picture book) by The Walt Disney Company	£1.75
The Ghostbusters Story Book by Anne Digby	£2.50
Cry Vampire (fiction) by Terrance Dicks	£1.50
Nellie and the Dragon (fiction) by Elizabeth Lindsay	£1.75
Aliens in the Family (fiction) by Margaret Mahy	£1.50
Voices (fiction) by Joan Aiken	£1.95
Cheerleaders Summer Special (fiction)	£2.95
My First Christmas Activity Book by Donna Bryant	£2.50
Sleuth (activity) by Sherlock Ransford	£1.50
Modern Disasters (non-fiction) by Jane Ferguson	£1.95
The Spooktacular Joke Book by Theodore Freek	£1.25
Stupid Cupid (joke book) by Trudie Hart	£1.75

You'll find these and many more great Hippo books at your
local bookshop, or you can order them direct. Just send off to
*Customer Services, Hippo Books, Westfield Road, Southam,
Leamington Spa, Warwickshire CV33 0JH*, not forgetting to
enclose a cheque or postal order for the price of the book(s)
plus 30p per book for postage and packing.